ALFIE ~THE~ WEREWOLF

ALFIE THE WEREWOLF
Werewolf Secrets

Written by
Paul van Loon

Translated by
David Colmer

Illustrated by
Hugo van Look

Hodder
Children's
Books

A division of Hachette Children's Books

First published in The Netherlands under the title *Weerwolfgeheimen*
by Uitgeverij Leopold in 1996
Published by arrangement with Rights People, London

First published in Great Britain in 2011 by Hodder Children's Books

The publishers are grateful for the support of the
Dutch Foundation for Literature.

1

A Catalogue record for this book is available from the British Library

ISBN 978 0 340 98983 8

Typeset in Weiss by Avon DataSet Ltd,
Bidford on Avon, Warwickshire

Printed and bound in Great Britain by
CPI Bookmarque Ltd, Croydon, Surrey

The paper and board used in this paperback by Hodder Children's Books
are natural recyclable products made from wood grown in
sustainable forests. The manufacturing processes conform to the
environmental regulations of the country of origin.

Hodder Children's Books
a division of Hachette Children's Books
338 Euston Road, London NW1 3BH
An Hachette UK Company
www.hachette.co.uk

For Richard

1

A Mystery House

'Holidays!' Alfie yelled as he leapt out of the bedroom window. He rolled down the cottage roof, dropped over the edge and fell to the ground with a whoosh. High above him he could see stars and the full moon.

'*Wrow*, Noura, what's taking so long?'

'*Wraa!* I'm coming.' The next instant Noura landed on all fours next to Alfie. They grinned at each other, then ran into the forest.

'*Wrow*, it's beautiful here,' Alfie growled. He already looked a little wolfish, with pointy ears and hairy hands. Noura nodded. She was changing too. Her nose had turned into a black snout.

'It's a great place for a holiday. And fantastic I could come with you.'

Alfie nodded. 'Grandpa Werewolf said we should come here: Mum and Dad, and Tim and me, and you too. He used to come here for his holidays when he was a young werewolf.' In the distance Alfie saw the crest of a hill sticking up over the treetops. 'I'll race you to the top of that hill! I bet I beat you.'

Noura laughed. 'We'll see about that.'

Alfie shot off, zigzagging between the trees, and Noura raced after him. They leapt over thick trunks with ease, their shadows danced in the moonlight and leaves swirled up in the air. As Alfie and Nora ran, they changed more and more. Hands turned into paws with sharp claws. Noses and mouths turned into hairy snouts and muzzles. By the time they reached the foot of the hill, Alfie and Noura

2

had transformed completely. They were all werewolf.

'*Wrow*, can you keep up, Noura?'

'*Wraa!* No problem, Alfie. Can *you* keep up with *me*?' Noura tore off up the hill. Alfie laughed, ran after her and overtook her again. First one was in the lead, then the other. Sometimes Alfie was looking back laughing. The next minute, Noura was winking at *him* over *her* shoulder.

Finally they reached the top of the hill neck and neck, threw their heads back and howled at the moon. 'Woo-woo-woo!'

'You won, Noura.'

'No, I didn't. You were first.'

Alfie pointed. 'Look, over there!'

The pointy roof of a big dark building was visible beyond the trees.

'*Wrow*, a mystery house! Shall we go and have a look?'

'Are you brave enough, Alfie? Maybe it's a ghost house.'

Alfie hesitated for a moment. The house looked deserted and derelict. The kind of

4

place ghosts would feel right at home in, he thought.

'Of course, I'm brave enough, Noura. Maybe there are ghosts, but so what? We're werewolves, aren't we? Come on.'

Cautiously they followed the path up to the front door. The night seemed to grow quieter and quieter. Bats fluttered around the chimney and the moon hung in the sky like an enormous searchlight shining down on the windows. The house was sagging, as if it was old and tired.

Alfie took Noura by the paw and felt her sharp claws prick his skin. The hair on her fingers tickled his werewolf skin.

'Who do you think lived here, Noura?'

'I haven't got a clue,' Noura said. 'Or maybe I do. I think it was Count Dracula, the famous vampire.'

'*Wrow!* I thought he lived in Transylvania or somewhere like that.' Giggling, Alfie climbed the stone steps to the front door, turned the doorknob and pushed. The door wasn't locked. Creaking, it swung open . . .

2

Footsteps

Behind the door was a long, seemingly endless hall. The moon shone in through tall windows, casting squares and rectangles of light on the floor.

'*Wrow*, mysterious,' Alfie said.

'There's nothing mysterious about it,' Noura said. 'It's just an old empty house.' She looked around. 'It smells really ancient in here. Like an old people's home. And that's not very exciting. Shall we go?'

'Wait. I know a fun game.' Alfie stood on a square of light. Noura stood next to him and held his hand.

'Jump!' Alfie said, and they jumped through the darkness to land on the next square of light, their toe claws clicking on the tiles as they jumped from one to the next.

In the exact middle of the hall was a door with a sign on it.

WSO
No Unauthorized Entry

'What's WSO mean?' Noura asked.

Alfie shrugged. 'No idea, but I think we're *unauthorized*.'

There were paintings hanging left and right of the door, portraits of men and women. The men all had striking sideburns, and so did the women!

'They look very strict,' Noura whispered.

'Maybe *they're* authorized,' Alfie sniggered.

'Shhh,' Noura hissed suddenly. 'Did you hear that?'

Alfie listened. Something creaked in the distance. *Creak.*

'It's nothing, Noura. Old houses always creak.'

Again there was a creaking sound, but closer this time, coming from the end of the hall. Then a cough. Footsteps: *Stomp, stomp!* It sounded like someone was coming up from a cellar. Noura gave Alfie a questioning look.

'Do old houses cough and stomp too?'

Alfie shook his head. 'I . . . I don't think so.'

'Then we'd better hide . . . quick,' Noura whispered.

'*Wrow*, in here? Even though we're not authorized?'

Noura just nodded. Alfie pressed down the handle and the door opened.

'Come on.'

Quickly they slipped inside. Alfie closed the door carefully and listened.

The footsteps in the hall grew louder.
Stomp, stomp!

'At least it's not a ghost,' Alfie whispered.
'Ghosts don't stamp their feet. They float
along without a sound.'

The footsteps stopped at the door.
Alfie held his breath.
The handle moved.
Alfie's eyes flashed
round the room,
spotting a big
w o o d e n
chair with
solid legs.

'Q u i c k ,
Noura, over
there!'

The door
s q u e a k e d
s l i g h t l y
open just
as Noura
and Alfie
dived behind

9

the chair. Alfie peered around the back of the chair and saw a dark, shadowy face in the doorway.

'Are you in here?' the stranger snarled.

3

The Secret Room

The door opened further. *Stomp, stomp!* Alfie and Noura crept under the chair. Again they heard the angry voice – much louder this time.

'Mooma doesn't like practical jokes.'

It was clearly a woman's voice and from the sound of it she was standing right next to them.

'You know the agreement. No sneaking around in the Secret Room. Otherwise Mooma will get in trouble with the WSO. And Mooma wouldn't like that!'

Alfie screwed up his eyes. *Stomp, stomp!* It sounded as if the woman was walking around the room. He felt Noura's paw on his arm.

'If you break the rules, you deserve to be punished!'

Stomp, stomp!

'And you know what that means! No full moon outing tonight. No, no, no. You'll shiver in the icy cellar . . .'

Noura's claws dug into Alfie's arm, almost making him growl with pain. He forced himself to stay still and wait in silence.

'OK,' said the voice after a while. 'So there's no one here! But if Mooma finds out you were here after all . . . You'll catch it then, sweeties!'

Stomp, stomp, and the door slammed shut.

Alfie and Noura stayed motionless under the chair. It was only after a few minutes that Alfie dared move.

'*Wrow*, who was that?' he whispered. 'Who was she talking to? And who's Mooma? Is *she* Mooma?'

Noura shrugged. 'No idea. For a moment I thought she was talking to us.'

Alfie nodded. 'Me too. I was really relieved she wasn't, because she doesn't even know us. And we don't know her. I don't want to know her! She yells like a . . . big bully. And she's as big as an ox. I don't want to bump into her again. Let's get out of here fast!'

Noura didn't answer. She was looking around thoughtfully. The room had tall windows with long velvet curtains and semi-circular fanlights above them. The moon was shining in through a fanlight. Here too there were paintings of men and women on the walls.

'Look, Alfie. More authorized people.'

Alfie grinned.

'What's so secret about this room anyway? Is it those paintings or . . .' Noura stared at the wall opposite her. There were trees painted on it. Ten of them, with long thin branches reaching up to the ceiling. And there was something special about them.

13

There were little boxes painted on the branches and inside the boxes there were names. Next to some of the names there were photos.

'Hey, Alfie, see that?' Noura whispered. 'A wall covered with trees full of names and photos. Do you think they're pedigrees?'

'I don't even know what a pedigree is,' Alfie said. 'I just want to get out of here.'

'You know,' Noura explained. 'A family

14

tree. So you can see who you're descended from. I wonder whose—'

Alfie tugged on her arm. '*Wrow!* Come on, Noura. Just forget about the pedi-trees. That big ox could come back any minute.'

'Yes, but—'

'No time, Noura. We have to go!' Gently he pushed Noura out of the room. She looked back over her shoulder one last time, but Alfie quickly closed the door.

They were back in the dark hall. Alfie looked left and right, but couldn't see anyone. They couldn't hear any footsteps either.

'Let's go,' Alfie growled, running quickly to the front door. 'Hopefully she hasn't locked it.' Alfie grabbed the doorknob, turned and pushed. The door wouldn't budge. Shocked, he looked at Noura. 'Just what I was afraid of.'

At the other end of the hall a door squeaked.

'*Wrow*, she's coming. And the door won't open!'

4

A Tall Figure

Alfie pushed the door with his two front paws.

'*Wrow!* Open up, you stupid door.'

Noura glanced back. She heard a cough from the darkness at the far end of the hall. Then footsteps. *Stomp, stomp!*

'Out of the way, Alfie.' Noura laid a paw on the doorknob. 'You're not meant to push; you have to pull. Like this.'

The door swung open on the inside and a stripe of moonlight appeared at their feet. Alfie blushed.

'*Wrow*, stupid. I forgot.'

Quickly they ran out, leaping down the stone steps and sprinting along the path and into the shadows of the big trees.

'We're safe here,' Alfie growled. 'At least, I hope so.' Panting, he peered through the bushes at the house. They'd left the door open.

A dark figure suddenly appeared in the doorway. Wild, bushy hair and a big, square body, wrapped in a dressing gown. It moved

its head from left to right, eyes gleaming.

For a second Alfie thought that the eyes had seen him and were piercing the darkness to stare at him. He heard heavy snorting and growling. Suddenly the figure turned and went back inside, slamming the door behind it.

'Phew, that was close,' Alfie said. 'She looks like a big box on legs!'

Noura nodded. 'Let's just get back to the cottage.'

'*Wrow*, good idea. I'll have to tell Grandpa Werewolf about this house. Maybe he already knows about it. This could end up an exciting holiday!'

They turned and ran down the hill, further into the forest. The house was soon out of sight but they kept on running until they reached a small river that ran through the forest like a flowing silver ribbon. Panting, Alfie stopped, took off his glasses and wiped the lenses clean.

'Do you think that big box saw us, Noura?'

Noura puffed and tried to catch her breath.

'I . . . I don't think so. We got out of there pretty fast.'

Alfie nodded. 'That's what I thought too.'

They walked on, following the river. The murmuring of the water calmed Alfie down and made him forget about the bad-tempered woman.

'It was great your parents let you come, Noura.'

'Yeah, cool.' Noura grinned at him. 'Of course, they still don't know I'm a werewolf. I think they don't even believe in werewolves.'

'*Wrow*, if only they knew!'

Noura rubbed her muzzle thoughtfully. 'I wonder what those family trees were, with all those photos.'

Alfie growled. 'Who cares about a boring old pedi-tree? The forest is full of trees.'

Noura shrugged. 'I just love secrets, Alfie. Especially mysterious ones. They make me really curious.'

Alfie was only half listening. He'd suddenly got a strange feeling. A shiver ran down his back as if someone was watching him. He stopped and turned his head, then jumped.

Standing on the other side of the river, with its shadow falling on the water, was a tall figure. Bent forwards and a little bit crooked, with a pointy nose and a sharp chin. It just stood there: dark, motionless, menacing . . .

5

The Rock

'Pssst! Noura, look. There!' Alfie pointed at the dark figure, which still hadn't moved. It stood there like a statue in the light of the moon.

'What's that person doing over there?' Alfie whispered.

Noura stared across the river. 'I don't see anyone. Or do you mean that big rock?'

Alfie looked again more carefully, then slapped himself on the forehead. *Whack!* Of course, Noura was right. It was just a rock.

'*Wrow!* I'm being silly, Noura. I really

thought I could see someone.'

'It's OK, Alfie,' Noura said. 'Sometimes I see things that aren't there either.' She pointed at the clouds floating past the moon. 'Like mountains of ice cream.'

Alfie looked at the river. It was shallow here and fairly narrow with lots of flat stones in the water.

'I'll just have a look anyway.' He jumped

on to the first stone and then the next one. In no time he was on the opposite bank.

'Wait for me, Alfie. What are you doing?' Noura followed.

'I just want a better look at that rock.' Alfie moved closer. The rock was tall, round and pitch black.

It's just a big stone, thought Alfie. Why did I think someone was standing here? I'm going mad! He hesitated, then laid a paw on the rock. Immediately a strange sensation flooded through him. It felt like his insides were turning to ice. All at once he felt completely alone and very sad. So sad that it hurt.

He jerked his paw back with a cry.

6

A Song

'What's wrong?' Noura asked.

Dazed, Alfie looked at her. He felt that his cheeks were wet.

'I . . . I don't know, Noura. The rock made me feel really awful. All alone.' He shook his head. 'It was horrible. I've never felt anything like it!'

Noura stroked his head, leaning on the rock with her other paw. 'Is it over now?' Suddenly a shudder passed through her. She dropped to her knees and covered her face with her paws.

'Noura, what is it?' Alfie exclaimed. 'Do you feel it too?'

Noura's shoulders jerked. 'Pain in my heart,' she sobbed. 'Sorrow in my stomach.'

Alfie swallowed. 'That's what I felt too. But it's not real. It comes from the rock.'

Noura sighed deeply, wiped her eyes and stood up again. 'It's a . . . *weeping rock*.'

'Really?' said Alfie. 'I've never heard of anything like that.'

'I just made it up,' Noura said. 'A rock that makes you cry is a weeping rock.'

Alfie nodded. '*Wrow*, that's true.' He looked around and shivered. It felt so much colder all of a sudden.

'Maybe it's because of this spot. It's so quiet here. It's weird. You can't hear a thing.' He fell silent because suddenly he *could* hear something: a rustling, whispering sound coming from between the trees.

The wind whistled and the whistling turned into words and the words turned into a song.

Close to the bank of the Silver River
Where the windswept pine trees groan
There stands Armando now and for ever
Hear him sigh and hear him moan

The singing stopped and the wind died down. Silence. Noura scratched her head.

'What a strange song. Who was singing it?'

'That was a *song wind*,' Alfie said.

'Really? I've never heard of anything like that.'

'Yep. That's because *I* just made it up,' Alfie grinned. 'But this really is a strange place.'

Noura nodded. 'A weeping rock and a singing wind. Very strange! Let's go somewhere else.'

'*Song wind*,' said Alfie. 'I made it up so I know . . .'

Noura was staring past Alfie.

'*Wrow*. What is it, Noura?' He turned and saw figures emerging from the bushes. Jagged shadows in the moonlight. Heads

covered with fierce, spiky hair. Triangular
ears. Sharp snouts and hairy coats. Alfie and
Noura heard growls and whispers. Slowly
the figures crept closer. Tails swung back
and forth. Eyes gleamed in the darkness.
Alfie grabbed Noura's hand.

'Wolves!' said Noura. 'And they don't
look friendly!'

Alfie nodded. '*Wrow*, I'll count to three
and then we run. One, two . . .

7

Three!

'Three!'

Alfie and Noura tore off together, racing past trees and leaping over bushes. Alfie felt the wind ruffle his coat as Noura ran beside him. Behind them they heard growling. Ever closer.

'Faster, Noura,' Alfie growled. 'They're catching up.'

Straining twice as hard, they ran on. Alfie's tongue was hanging out of his mouth.

The pursuers fell behind. Further and

further. Alfie looked aside at Noura and smiled. Strangely enough, he suddenly felt fantastic. He'd almost forgotten about the mystery house and the weird rock. There was nothing he liked more than running through the woods, trees all around him and the full moon and stars overhead. It made him happy.

'This is a fun race too,' he growled. 'I bet we win!'

Noura looked back. 'I don't know, Alfie. They're catching up again and I'm getting tired.'

Suddenly she stopped.

'*Wrow*, what are you doing?' Alfie growled, stopping as well. 'Come on, Noura, keep running! Otherwise they'll catch up with us and then we won't win.'

Noura shook her head. An angry crease appeared over her eyes. She crossed her arms.

'I've had enough. I don't need to win. Why should we run away from those wolves? We're werewolves after all. We're like cousins to wolves. I can't be bothered being scared.'

The pursuers' horrible growls were getting closer and closer. Noura stood in the middle of the path, spread her legs wide and planted her feet firmly on the ground.

'Don't do it, Noura,' Alfie growled.

Noura ignored him. She raised one paw.

'*Wraa!* STOP!'

8

Pile-up

'*Wrow*, Noura, what are you doing?' Alfie could already see the first pursuer racing around the corner. Noura was standing on the path like a traffic policeman signalling the cars to stop. Her eyes blazed.

'STOP,' she growled again.

'No!' Alfie cried, hurling himself in front of Noura. Shocked and trying to slow down, the front wolf tripped over a tree root and did a somersault. Sand, leaves and branches flew through the air. The wolf landed flat on its stomach right in front of Alfie.

'Ooph!' it groaned. Almost straightaway another wolf fell and landed on top of it. SMACK! Then, one after the other, all of the pursuers crashed into each other. BOF! THUNK! SPLAT! WHAM! KLUNK!

It was a wolf pile-up. They flew over each, whizzed through the air and crashed down until the whole troop was lying on the ground, groaning and growling. Legs and

tails were tangled together. Some of the wolves had gone cross-eyed from the impact.

Alfie quickly counted them. There were six. They don't actually look that dangerous any more, he thought. Especially not with their eyes crossed like that.

'What did you do that for?' Noura asked.

'*Wrow*, er, I . . . I was trying to protect you.'

Noura looked at the pile of dazed wolves. 'You did a good job of it, then. It was sweet of you, Alfie, but it really wasn't necessary. I wasn't scared, you know.'

The wolves shook their heads and struggled to untangle their tails and legs.

'What do you want from us?' Alfie demanded.

The wolves growled and snarled amongst themselves, then looked back at Alfie and Noura. They seemed to have something to say.

Then something strange happened. One after the other they stood up on their hind legs. Only now did Alfie notice: the wolves were all wearing dark-grey tracksuits with the letters WWW on them.

Wolves in clothes! That could only mean one thing.

'*Wrow!* You mean you're werewolves too?'

The biggest wolf cleared his throat. 'Arrgh, ahum. I'm Igor.' He gestured at the others. 'That's Olga, Nelson, Kim Li, Inouk and Ashanti.'

In turn each of the werewolves growled a greeting. Noura raised an eyebrow in anger.

'Why were you chasing us?' she snapped.

Igor shrugged, twisted his mouth and gave a growling snigger. 'It was a game. We wanted to play with you. We never see any other kids, let alone werewolf kids. We thought you'd like it . . .'

'Really? Is that what you thought?' Noura said. 'Well, you were wrong!'

'You've got really nice hair,' one of the girl werewolves said, and Noura's angry expression disappeared immediately.

'Really?'

The girl werewolf nodded. 'Definitely.

I'm Olga.' She held out a paw.

'Noura,' Noura said, shaking paws.

Alfie could hardly believe it. So many werewolves in one spot . . .

Igor growled. 'We thought you might like to be our friends.'

'*Wrow*, werewolf friends; that sounds good to me,' Alfie growled. 'It's pretty cool actually and—'

Suddenly there was a bloodcurdling howl. The six werewolves looked up in

fright. The howl sounded angry, terrifying and sorrowful all at once. It was coming from the direction of the house on the hill.

'Mooma,' Igor whispered. 'She's found out that we've escaped out of our rooms.'

'Mooma? Who's that?' Alfie asked.

Igor looked at him with trembling ears. 'The head. We have to go!'

The werewolves turned and ran off, ignoring Alfie and Noura.

'Igor, Olga, wait,' Noura shouted. 'What does WWW mean?'

The werewolves kept running without looking back and in just a few seconds they'd disappeared in the darkness.

Alfie and Noura stared in astonishment at the empty spot where six werewolves had stood a moment before, then looked at each other.

'Too bad,' Noura said. 'We almost made some werewolf friends. Strange, them just running off like that.'

'*Wrow!*' Alfie said. 'Maybe we'll see them again tomorrow. We've had enough strange things for one night. I'm tired.'

They ran back to the cottage, where they climbed up the drainpipe and over the window ledge into Alfie's bedroom. The moment he saw his bed, Alfie started yawning.

'Ah-wahhh, good night, Noura.'

'Goodnight, Alfie,' Noura laughed, softly closing the door behind her. Alfie flopped down on to his bed.

This is going to be a fun holiday, he thought, stretching his arms and extending his claws. There's a mystery house, a troop of young werewolves, a weeping rock and a song wind! Does Grandpa Werewolf know? Maybe that's why he sent us here.

That was as far as his thoughts went, because the next second Alfie was sleeping like a log.

Friendly werewolves appeared in his dream, wanting to play with him. But suddenly there was a great big one, singing at the top of her voice.

I'm the ox, the great big box
The great big, big-bad bully box
I'll grab you, I'll nab you
I'll squeeze you, I'll squash you
And wring you out like sweaty socks

Alfie shot up in bed with sweat running down his back. The sun was shining into his room and outside the birds were singing.

He looked at his hand. The fur and claws were gone. It was morning and he was back to being an ordinary boy.

9
Sculpturer

Late in the morning, Alfie walked into the kitchen, still feeling a bit wolfish. Noura was already sitting at the table and Alfie noticed that she too had a fierce look about her. Her hair was tangled and there was a pale-yellow gleam in her eyes. They were often like that when it was full moon, because that was when Alfie and Noura changed into werewolves for three nights in a row, and sometimes you could still see a remnant of it in the daytime. Especially when they'd had a long, wild night.

Tim joined them looking like he'd had an excellent night's sleep. That was because Tim wasn't a werewolf who goes out under the full moon at night. Tim was Alfie's best friend and Tim's dad was standing at the stove.

'Good morning, sleepyheads,' he called, looking over his shoulder and winking.

Tim's parents had adopted Alfie. They'd even done it after they'd found out that he was a werewolf. Alfie was crazy about them and they loved Alfie just as much as they loved Tim.

Dad was wearing blue overalls, an apron and grass-green wellies. On his head he had a tea cosy shaped like an elephant. Dad loved being 'different'.

'Sit down, boys. The pancakes are ready.'

Dad had been hard at work with the frying pan and a bowl of batter, and the kitchen smelt delicious. Carefully he carried an enormous pile of pancakes over to the table on a plate.

'Look at this,' he said proudly. 'It's a real

work of art. It's wonkier than the Leaning Tower of Pisa and almost as high. But a lot yummier.'

Alfie sat down next to Noura and whispered, 'I'd rather have a raw steak.'

Noura laughed quietly. Alfie could see that her teeth were still a little pointy.

'Dig in, kids.'

Dad took off the apron and walked over to the worktop to pick up a special belt with all kinds of pouches and loops. It was his tool belt and it was full of chisels, knives and a hammer. Dad buckled it around his hips and winked.

'Cool, I look like a cowboy.' Then he put on a backpack. 'There. Now I'm going hunting. Will you tidy up afterwards?'

Alfie looked up with surprise.

'You going hunting, Dad?' Tim asked. 'What for?'

'Not for rabbits or deer, I hope,' said Noura. 'That'd be cruel. Even as a werewolf I wouldn't want to hurt a poor little bunny.'

Dad smiled. 'No, of course not, sweetie. I'm going hunting for rocks. My hands are itching. My hammer and chisels can't wait. I want to start hacking, so I'm going out to look for a really beautiful one. Grandpa Werewolf said that this forest is wonderful for sculpturers.'

Alfie looked up. 'Really? Did Grandpa Werewolf say that?'

Dad nodded. 'He said, "There are very beautiful rocks." So I'm going looking for them. I've been feeling very artistic lately. We artists are like that. Inspiration can hit us at any moment. So there's no time to lose. Bye!'

Astonished, Alfie stared at the closed door.

'Artist?' he said. 'Since when?'

Tim smiled. 'You know what Dad's like.

He's crazy about change. He's started calling himself a sculpturer.'

'A sculpturer?' said Noura. 'You mean a sculptor?'

Tim grinned. 'No, Dad's different. He's a sculpturer.'

Alfie smiled. 'OK. Let's have breakfast before the sculpturer's pancakes get cold.'

While they were eating, Alfie told Tim what had happened that night.

'Other werewolves?' Tim said. 'Cool!'

'Yeah,' said Noura. 'Except they ran off really fast.'

'Oh, tough,' said Tim.

Alfie took a big bite of pancake. 'Mmm, this is as yummy as raw steak after all.' Still chewing, he looked at Tim. 'When's Mum coming?'

Tim shrugged. 'Not till tomorrow, I think. She's come down with a virus.'

'Really, what's she got?'

'A cleaning virus. She wanted to give the house a good scrub first.' He stuffed a piece of pancake into his mouth and swallowed it whole. 'And apparently that's a lot easier with us out of the way. Lucky for us we got to come on holiday early.'

Alfie sniggered and pushed his plate away.

They were just clearing the table when they heard brakes squeal outside, followed by a dull thud and some rattling.

10

Surprise

'That's the Dentmobile,' Tim shouted happily. 'Mum's here.'

They all ran outside, where a small yellow Fiat was crunched up against a tree. The damage wasn't too bad as far as they could tell. It was just a little dent in the bumper. You didn't even notice it, because of all the other dings and dents at the front, the sides and the back. Even the roof was bent. That was why Tim and Alfie called the car the Dentmobile. Mum had got her driving licence back just a few weeks before.

The door swung open and Mum climbed out with a bag slung over her shoulder. She smiled at the tree.

'Sorry,' she said. 'I thought you'd get out of the way.' She rummaged through her bag, found a plaster to stick on the tree, then spread her arms to hug the three children.

'Hi, sweethearts. Grandpa Werewolf talked me into coming sooner. Keeping a house tidy is important, but I'm glad to be here with you.' She studied the cottage approvingly. 'What a great little holiday home! Good thinking of Grandpa Werewolf to send us here. It really is beautiful. Although I've heard you can get a lot of rain here too. And thunderstorms.'

'We haven't noticed, Mum,' said Alfie. 'We haven't had a drop of rain yet.'

Mum clapped her hands. 'All the better. And, um . . . Of course, I've brought a surprise for you.'

'Really?' said Alfie. 'What? I love surprises.'

'Me too,' said Tim.

Mum smiled. 'And what about you, Noura? Do you love surprises too?'

Noura nodded shyly. 'Yes, I quite like them.'

'Thought so,' Mum said. 'Have a look on the back seat.'

Tim, Alfie and Noura hurried over to the car and peered in through the side window. Hunched up on the back seat was a sleeping figure dressed in a hat and a raincoat and hugging a walking stick. The hat had a wide brim, but beneath it you could clearly see a black wolf's muzzle.

11

Snoring

'Grandpa Werewolf!' Alfie cried, pulling the door open. The figure on the back seat woke with a start and almost rolled out of the car. He grabbed hold of the seat just in time.

'What? Who? Where? Are we still alive? What a suicide jockey!' Grandpa Werewolf struggled up out of the car. 'Hi, Alfie, Tim, Noura.'

Alfie hugged him.

Grandpa was always a werewolf. He didn't have to wait for the full moon any more. That was something only very old werewolves could do, if they wanted to.

'How was the trip, Grandpa?' Alfie asked politely. He was actually bursting with impatience and dying to ask him something else. Grandpa Werewolf yawned with gaping jaws.

'O-wahhh, I survived, Alfie. I'm glad of that. But that mother of yours was snoring the whole way. That was a pain, because it kept me awake.'

'Oh. Can I ask you—'

Mum started laughing. 'I'm afraid you're mistaken, Grandpa Werewolf. I wasn't snoring! I was at the wheel! You can't drive and snore at the same time.'

Alfie cleared his throat very loudly.

'Er-hmmm! Do you know that house on—'

'I still heard snoring the whole time,' Grandpa mumbled. 'I swear it on the grave of my own werewolf grandfather!'

Mum grinned. 'Maybe *you* were the one who was snoring.'

Grandpa Werewolf shook his head. 'I

don't believe that for an instant. It was someone else.'

Mum looked at Alfie, raised her eyebrows and winked. 'Oh well, why don't you go and have a nice nap now, Grandpa Werewolf?'

No! thought Alfie. There's something I want to find out first.

Grandpa picked up his walking stick.

'I'll do that,' he mumbled. 'I have to make sure I'm fit later, because all kinds of things still need to happen.'

Alfie tugged on Grandpa's coat. 'Grandpa, do you know anything about a mysterious house and—'

Grandpa Werewolf looked back. 'No, Alfie. At the moment I don't know anything. I want to have a good sleep first.'

The old werewolf turned and stomped into the holiday home.

12

A Tent

'Did you see that? Grandpa Werewolf wouldn't even listen to me.'

Alfie was walking through the wood with Tim and Noura. Birds were singing and squirrels were running along branches. Mum was having a rest in the cottage and Grandpa Werewolf had lain down on the sofa and gone straight to sleep.

'He's not usually that grumpy,' Tim said. 'But I understand. Everyone's always exhausted after a ride in Mum's Dentmobile.'

Alfie and Noura sniggered.

After a while they came out at the river. The sun was shining on the water, which was glittering like silver and splashing merrily against the banks.

'What are we going to do today?' Noura asked. Alfie took off his glasses and wiped the lenses.

'Shall we go and have another look at that house on the hill? There's something mysterious going on there. If you ask me it's got something to do with those other werewolves.'

'Yeah, and there's that Secret Room with mysterious family trees on the wall,' said Noura.

'Good idea,' Tim said. 'I'll come with you. I love mysteries.'

'Let's go,' Noura said, running off towards the hill. Tim and Alfie raced along behind her, but suddenly Noura stopped.

There was a big white tent on the bank of the river. 'Hey, look over there. Who do you think that is?'

As they moved closer they saw signs.

'What's all that about?' Tim asked.

Alfie shrugged. 'There wasn't any tent here last night.'

Cautiously they circled the tent. Someone on the inside cast a moving shadow on the material. Signs at the back and sides of the tent said GO AWAY!

'Strange,' Noura whispered. 'Wasn't this where the weeping rock was? Where's it gone? And who set up the tent?'

Suddenly they heard clanging, chiselling noises inside the tent. Then a loud cry. 'Arghhh!'

13

Not Sad

'Help, what's happening in that tent?' Alfie whispered. 'Is someone getting killed in there or what?'

'Maybe it's a dentist's tent,' Tim grinned. 'With someone getting drilled.'

Alfie looked at him with surprise. 'You think so?'

Alfie had such a strange expression on his face that Tim burst out laughing.

'I'm just joking, Alfie.'

Noura punched him on the shoulder.

'Ow,' Tim cried. 'You can see it's full moon

again. You're always a lot stronger then.'

'Sorry.'

'It's OK. But, um, I think I know who's in the tent. If you ask me it's—'

'Shhh,' Alfie said. 'Quiet. I can hear something.'

Suddenly someone unzipped the tent. An elephant emerged, with a head under it.

'Dad!' Alfie exclaimed.

Dad's face was red and a tear was rolling out of the corner of his eye. He looked

around with a confused expression.

'Dad, what's wrong?' Tim exclaimed. 'What are you doing in that tent?'

Dad blinked. 'That . . . is none of your business. I'm making art here. That requires silence and solitude. So you have to go away.'

'But why are you crying?' Noura asked. Dad wiped his eyes and held up his thumb.

'My thumb. I hit it with the hammer. But I'm perfectly fine. I'm happy. I'm not sad. I've found a beautiful rock and I'm hacking away at it.'

Tim stepped forward. 'Can we have a look, Dad? How—'

'Stop!' Dad shouted. 'Go back! Nobody's allowed to see my work of art before it's finished.' His head disappeared and he zipped the tent back up. 'Go away, all of you! I have to work.'

Alfie looked at the tent. He heard the sound of the hammer and chisel. *Clink! Clack!* Iron on stone. And a sob every now and then.

Suddenly a gust of wind rustled their hair. In that gust there was a scrap of song:

Long, long ago, Armando was young
In love with life, in love with blood . . .

The ghostly song drifted off between the trees.

'Did you hear that?' Alfie whispered.

Noura nodded. 'Just like last night!'

'What?' said Tim. 'What did you hear?'

14
A Voice

'It was the song wind,' Alfie explained. 'It was singing a strange song, but now it's gone.'

Noura stared into the distance as if she could see the wind drifting off between the trees. 'Just like last night!'

Tim screwed up his eyes. 'Song wind? I don't get to see anything and now I can't hear anything either.'

Alfie scratched his elbow. 'Maybe the wind only sings for werewolf ears.'

'Humph, a werewolf-ears-only wind!

That's not fair.'

'It's not our fault,' Alfie said.

Noura nodded. 'It's a weird song anyway. About some guy called Armando. It doesn't mean a thing to us.'

'Aargh!'

The cry came from inside the tent. *Zzrrripp!* Again Dad's head appeared.

'I can't concentrate with all your talking. I just bashed my thumb again. Will you please just go away?' He looked at them sadly while wiping away another tear from the corner of his eye. 'Go on!' Dad's head disappeared and the zip went back up again. *Zzrrripp!*

Tim looked at Alfie and Noura. 'Come on, let's go somewhere else. Dad isn't quite himself today.'

They tiptoed away, not daring to speak again until they were out of sight of the tent.

'It's weird though,' Alfie said. 'Dad's never this unfriendly. And he seems a bit sad too.'

Noura hadn't said anything for a while, as

if she was thinking about other things, but suddenly her eyes lit up.

'I know what it is!'

Alfie looked at her with confusion. 'What?'

Noura clapped her hands and did a little jig. 'Your dad found the weeping rock and put the tent up around it. But now he feels the sadness from the rock, just like we did. That's why he's acting so strange and sad. He's sculpturing the rock.'

Tim shook his head. 'A weeping rock? I suppose that's like the song wind, for werewolves only.'

'No, I don't think so,' Alfie said. 'It's really bothering Dad, so he must feel it too. And he's no werewolf, no matter how much he'd love to be one.'

Tim shrugged. 'Let him figure it out for himself then. He's sent us off, so there's nothing we can do to help.'

In the meantime they'd climbed to the top of the hill.

'Look, Tim,' Alfie whispered. 'See that

roof sticking up above the trees? That's the mystery house.'

They walked closer until they could see it clearly. In daylight the house even looked mysterious.

'Cool,' Tim said. 'Time for a thorough investigation. And we're the house inspectors.'

'Don't!' said a voice behind them.

15

Olga

Startled, they spun around and saw a girl with long blonde hair. She had light-blue eyes and was looking at Noura.

'Hi, Noura,' she said.

Alfie stared at the girl with surprise. 'Huh? Who are you? How do you know Noura's name?'

'Yeah, how *do* you know it?' asked Noura.

The girl smiled. 'I recognize your hairclips. You were wearing them last night too. We saw each other right here. Remember?' She looked at Alfie. 'I recognize your glasses too.

You were that cute little white werewolf, right? I'm Olga.'

'Cute? Me? Um . . . I'm . . . Alfie,' Alfie stuttered, his glasses misting over. 'Wait a sec.' He took off his glasses, wiped the lenses and put them back on. 'So you're one of the werewolves from last night.'

Olga smiled. 'Yes, just like you.'

Tim was staring at Olga, his eyes wide and with a red blush on his cheeks.

'Er . . . hello,' he said. 'I'm, um . . . Timothy!'

Olga smiled sweetly at him and Tim blushed even more.

'Are you a werewolf too, Timothy?' Olga asked.

'No, sorry. I'm—'

Noura interrupted him. 'So, Olga, what's the story with you and all those other werewolves? First you wanted to play with us, then all of a sudden you ran off. Why?'

'It's hard to explain, Noura.'

They sat down on the grass. Olga really did have extremely blonde hair and very light-blue eyes.

'Where do you come from, Olga?' Alfie asked.

'Denmark. We all come from different countries.'

Tim stared at Olga with dreamy eyes and his chin resting on his hands. 'So you're a werewolf too? How fascinating!' He rubbed his chin. 'You know . . . I'm actually an expert when it comes to werewolves. Some of my best friends are werewolves, so—'

Alfie nudged him with his elbow.

'Stop showing off, Tim-o-thy!' he whispered.

Olga smiled at Tim again. 'That's nice. Maybe we'll end up being best friends too, Timothy.'

Alfie saw Tim turning bright red yet again. Olga winked at him and he giggled quietly.

'Shhh,' Noura hissed, glaring at both Tim and Alfie. 'Babies!' Then she turned back to Olga. 'Why are you all from different countries, Olga?'

'We're orphans,' Olga explained. 'Werewolf orphans. Igor comes from Russia,

Kim Li from China, Nelson from Africa, Ashanti from India and Inouk comes from the North Pole.'

'Wow, that's cool!' Tim said.

Alfie sat up straight. 'Hey, I'm a kind of werewolf orphan too. But lucky for me I've got the best foster parents in the world, Tim's mum and dad.'

Tim put an arm around Alfie's shoulders.

Olga shook her head sadly. 'You're lucky, Alfie. Not like us. None of us have foster parents. No one wanted us. That's why the Organization picked us up.'

'The what?' Tim said.

'The Organization!' Olga pointed at her grey tracksuit with the letters WWW on it. 'Worldwide Werewolf Waifs. They pick up werewolf orphans all over the world and bring them to live in Mooma's werewolf orphanage.'

Alfie's mouth dropped and Tim stared at Olga with big eyes.

'A werewolf orphanage?' said Alfie. 'You mean that big house?'

Olga nodded. 'Yes, that's where Mooma and the werewolf orphans live. There's been a werewolf orphanage here for hundreds of years.'

Alfie looked at Noura. He could tell they were both thinking the same thing. Mooma? The Big Box?

He swallowed. 'Um, Olga. I've got a question. Actually I've got two. No, wait, maybe three! Who's Mooma?'

Olga sighed. 'She used to be nice to us, but now . . .'

Suddenly a gust of wind came out of the forest, rustling the bushes and making Alfie's hair stand up on end. He looked up in fright.

16

Talking

Olga turned pale and looked around with frightened eyes. Alfie followed her gaze. Was there something moving in the bushes? Something dark slid past. Or was it just the shadow of a cloud?

The wind died down again and the leaves of the bushes stopped rustling. The sun lit up the paths. Olga sighed, clearly relieved.

Phew, thought Alfie, it was nothing.

'I'm not supposed to talk about it,' Olga whispered. 'Mooma doesn't like us to! I'm not even supposed to be here. We're being punished.'

'Punished? What for?' asked Alfie.

'For running off into the forest last night. We didn't have permission. That's why we have to freeze in the icy cellar today. The others are all sitting there shivering, but I sneaked off.'

'Can you get back into the cellar without being seen?' Alfie asked.

Olga nodded. 'There's a secret trapdoor under the bushes. We use it when we want to sneak out. But not too often, otherwise Mooma would notice.'

Alfie cleared his throat. 'Um . . . Who's Mooma?'

Olga looked at him and sighed. 'Mooma runs the werewolf orphanage. She's a werewolf too. And she's very strict!'

Noura nudged Alfie. 'We saw her. Mooma. When we were in the house.'

Alfie nodded. 'The Big Box! I was scared to death!'

Olga looked at him quizzically. 'Are

69

you scared of boxes?'

'No,' said Alfie. 'Big Box is what I call—'

Crack! Somewhere behind them a branch snapped. Olga jumped up.

'I have to go,' she said.

'Wait!'

'I can't!' Olga's eyes darted left and right. 'I have to hurry back now, before Mooma finds out I'm gone.' She hesitated for a moment, looking at Tim and Alfie. 'I've got an idea. Shall we meet again tonight? Here? If I can sneak off again?'

Alfie gave her the thumbs-up. 'OK! Good plan, Olga.'

Olga waved, ran back to the big house and disappeared into the bushes. Tim gave a deep sigh, and so did Alfie. Noura didn't say a word.

On the way back they hardly spoke. Alfie couldn't stop thinking about the Organization. What if the Organization had come for him before Tim's parents took him in? He would have been living in Mooma's werewolf orphanage too. Alfie shuddered.

Then he thought of something else. If the werewolf orphanage is *really* old, Grandpa Werewolf must know about it too . . .

It wasn't long before they had arrived back at Dad's tent, where they heard furious hammering and chiselling.

'Wow,' said Alfie. 'Dad's really getting into it. I wonder what it's going to be.'

They stood there for a while listening. Between the hacking sounds, they heard quiet mumbling. Alfie looked at Noura.

'Who's Dad talking to?' He walked up to the tent and pressed his ear against the material. Tim and Noura did the same. They could make out Dad's voice clearly. He sounded cheerful.

'Don't worry. I'll get you out all right . . . What's that? No, don't be silly! You're a beautiful rock, so you're bound to be a magnificent statue. Just leave that to this old sculpturer.'

71

Noura looked at Alfie. 'He's talking to the rock!'

Alfie nodded. 'And you know what's really strange? Dad thinks the rock is talking back!'

17
Don't Worry

The hacking stopped. Tim gestured, Get down! And they all dropped to the ground.

Dad stepped out of the tent, turning back for a moment to say, 'Relax. I'm not leaving you alone. I'm just getting a bit of fresh air.'

Alfie noticed that his hands were black and his overalls filthy. Dad looked around and took a deep breath, then suddenly shouted, 'Yeah, yeah, I'm coming, OK! You're the most impatient hunk of rock I've ever met!' He hurried back into the tent.

73

Alfie stood up. 'Did you hear that?' he whispered.

Noura giggled.

'We better tell Mum,' Tim said. 'Maybe we need to call a doctor.'

'So Dad's talking to a rock?' Mum looked at Tim, Alfie and Noura for a moment, then burst out laughing. Tears sprang from her eyes. She held on to the table to keep from falling over. She quickly sat down on a chair and wiped the tears from her cheeks.

'It's really nothing to worry about. You know what Dad's like! Sometimes he wears a dress. Or flippers. The next thing you know he's walking around with a flowerpot on his head. If he's not wearing his elephant tea cosy of course. Not so long ago he suddenly started playing the accordion and now he's talking to a rock. It's brilliant, isn't it? That's him all over. There's absolutely nothing the matter. Dad just loves being different. Because being ordinary is so . . . ordinary. That's why I love him.'

'But the rock,' Alfie said. 'It's a weeping rock. It makes you sad. And he won't even let us into the tent to have a look.'

'What's that I hear?' With a groan, Grandpa Werewolf sat up on the sofa. He'd just woken up. He slid his hat back and stared at Alfie. 'Did I hear correctly? Were you talking about a sad rock?'

Alfie nodded. 'Yes, Grandpa. There's a rock close to the—'

Quietly the old werewolf growled the words Alfie had heard before. 'Close to the bank of the Silver River where the windswept pine trees groan . . .'

Alfie's mouth dropped. 'I know that song.'

'Me too,' exclaimed Noura.

'Not me,' said Tim in a sad voice.

Grandpa Werewolf slid back and forth on the sofa until he was comfortable, then rested his paws on the knob of his walking stick. Thoughtfully he stared out the window.

'That's the song of Armando the Grey. Only werewolves can hear it because . . .

Because it's an old werewolf story.'

It was deathly still in the room, with all eyes fixed on Grandpa Werewolf. But Grandpa didn't say another word. He just stared, unseeing, into the distance.

'Grandpa,' Alfie whispered, 'who's Armando the Grey?'

18

The Story of Armando the Grey

Grandpa Werewolf gave a deep sigh and looked at Alfie.

'The story of Armando the Grey is a long story, and it's an old story too. The river knows his name, the trees know his sorrow and the wind sings his song.'

'Was Armando a werewolf?' Alfie asked.

Grandpa Werewolf shook his head. 'Armando the Grey was a vampire, but he was a harmless vampire because he didn't have any fangs. A clever dentist pulled them out.'

'That's sad,' Tim said. 'At least, for a vampire it must have been.'

Grandpa Werewolf nodded. 'But that's another story. Armando's real sorrow came from something else. Armando was in love with a lady werewolf. It was an impossible love. A vampire and a werewolf don't belong together.'

'Why not?' Alfie asked.

Grandpa Werewolf shrugged. 'That's what they thought in the old days. It was forbidden. So Armando ended up alone. They say that the Silver River arose from the tears of Armando the Grey.'

'That's really sad,' Noura said. 'And romantic too. He must have cried so many tears.'

Grandpa Werewolf growled softly. 'Yes, it was hard on Armando, very hard. He went off to a dark place where the sun never shone and cried and cried. Day after day, week after week, year after year. And the Silver River arose at his feet.

'His sorrow was so great that he gradually turned to stone. His vampire heart became a lump of stone and so did he. In the end, Armando was gone. All that was left was a big black rock next to the river. And if you go near that rock, you feel Armando's sorrow.' Grandpa Werewolf sniffed and looked seriously at the three children. 'That is the story of Armando the Grey.'

'We saw a big black rock,' Alfie cried. 'At first we thought it was a person.'

'And we felt the sadness too,' Noura said. 'Great sadness.'

Grandpa Werewolf nodded slowly, almost approvingly, as if it was something he'd expected. 'Maybe you found Armando's rock.'

'And now Dad's hacking into it,' Tim blurted. 'Is that all right?'

Grandpa Werewolf gazed pensively at his walking stick. 'Maybe it will release the sorrow. That would be good. Then Armando would have peace at last.'

Mum had been listening silently the whole time. 'Goodness, what a story, Grandpa. But what happened to the werewolf he was in love with? She must have been very sad too.'

Grandpa Werewolf nodded. His eyes seemed to glaze over. 'I'll tell you about that another time. That's enough for now. I'm going to go out for a little walk to stretch my old legs. Bye!' Quickly he strode out of the cottage and down the path. Alfie ran along behind him.

'Wait, Grandpa. There's something else I'd like to ask you. Do you know anything about the Org—'

Grandpa Werewolf stopped suddenly next to the Dentmobile. He looked back and shook his head. 'Shhhh! D'you hear that, Alfie?'

Alfie listened. Now he could hear it too. Loud and clear: *Ghrrrr. Ghrrrr.*

Alfie and Grandpa Werewolf looked at the Dentmobile. The sound was coming from the boot . . .

19

An Unexpected Guest

Ghrrrr. Ghrrrr!

'Well, I'll be . . .' said Grandpa Werewolf. 'I was right all along!' He hit the boot with his stick, leaving one, two, three little round dents. 'Wake up, lazybones. And show yourself.'

Alfie was totally baffled. Tim and Noura had come to join him.

'Why is Grandpa Werewolf hitting the Dentmobile?' Noura asked. 'Is he angry about something?'

Tim shrugged.

'What do you mean, Grandpa?' Alfie asked.

Grandpa Werewolf smiled. 'I told you someone was snoring in the car. First I thought it was your mother. And she thought it was me, remember?'

Alfie nodded.

'Well,' he laughed, 'it wasn't either of us. It was an unexpected guest!' In one movement, Grandpa Werewolf opened the boot. The lid shot up and Alfie gaped at the boy who was lying there asleep. He was tall and skinny, with a sharp face, spiky hair and bushy eyebrows. His arms and legs were folded up like a grasshopper's and he was snoring loudly.

GHRRR. GHRRR!

'Leo!' Alfie cried.

'Exactly,' Grandpa Werewolf grinned. 'Now I know whose snoring was keeping me awake.'

'And he's still snoring,' Alfie said.

Grandpa Werewolf poked Leo in the ribs with his walking stick. 'Hey, steam engine. It's time to get up!'

The boy opened his eyes, saw Alfie and Grandpa Werewolf and gave a big grin.

'Cuz wolf!' he called out happily. 'It be youse! And it be Grandpa Werewolfy too. And Nourala and Timmio. Oh, happy daze!' He unfolded his arms and legs and crawled out of the boot. Standing up straight, he was almost two metres tall. Leo was Alfie's cousin. At full moon he turned into an enormous werewolf. He spread his arms. 'Hello, everyone-two-threes. Super-prize! Leo be here!' He wrapped his arms around Alfie.

'Whoa, Leo, wait!' Alfie shouted, but Leo was already throwing him up in the air. Leo was crazy about his cousin. Fortunately he caught him again.

'Put me down. Put me down,' Alfie shouted and Leo obeyed.

'Who now?' he grinned. 'Timmio? You wants to go flysing with Leo?'

Tim took a quick step back. 'No, thanks, Leo. Preferably not.'

Grandpa Werewolf smiled. 'Leo, you sneaky stowaway.'

Leo roared with laughter. 'Yes, Leo be a smartsy stopaway. He sneaked into the boots, then snored away lots of loverly hours. 'Cause Leo wants to go on holly days too with all the other holly day-makers.'

Grandpa Werewolf looked at him thoughtfully. 'Hmm, it's actually a good thing you're here. I think I might need a pair of strong hands later.'

Alfie looked at Grandpa Werewolf questioningly.

What does Grandpa mean by that? he wondered. What's going to happen later?'

'Hey, Grandpa, did you know there's an orph—'

Suddenly Leo nudged him.

'Hey-ho, Alfie wolf. Look there! Who be that appearifying out of nowheres? Who be that?'

Everyone looked around.

A pitch-black figure was coming up the garden path, shiny and gleaming like a piece of coal.

20

Father Christmas

Alfie, Noura and Tim stepped back.

'The weeping rock,' Alfie whispered. 'See. It's alive!'

The gleaming black man came closer. He clapped his hands and a cloud of black grit billowed up. A crescent of white teeth appeared in his black face.

'So, time for a sarnie.'

'Dad?' Tim and Alfie said in one voice.

'Yes, of course. Who did you think it was? Father Christmas?'

Leo laughed out loud. 'That's right, Dadsy.

You be Father Christmas and you be sitting in the chiminny too long.'

Grandpa Werewolf sniggered. 'You do look a bit like a coal miner. Have you been digging up some coal?' He rubbed his muzzle thoughtfully. 'Or, um, have you perhaps been working on a specially beautiful black rock?'

'Yes, why are you all black?' Noura asked.

Dad looked at his hands with surprise, as if he he'd only just noticed.

'Oh, that . . . that's from chiselling, I guess. I'm making a wonderful sculpture. And you're right, Grandpa, it is from a beautiful black rock. Art takes grit, sweat and tears. But now I have to eat something. I'm a little faint from hunger.'

Just then Mum came out of the house. She recognized Dad immediately.

'Ah, sweetheart, nice and black, I see. You must have been hard at work. Run along and have a shower.'

Dad shook his head. 'No time, no time,' he mumbled. 'A quick sandwich and then back to work. I promised I wouldn't be long.'

Mum looked at him with surprise. 'Who did you promise?'

Dad pulled a hankie out of his pocket and wiped his face, leaving a white stripe over his eyes and nose.

'The rock. The black rock. It's waiting for me. I said I'd be back soon.'

Grandpa Werewolf screwed up his eyes. 'Hmm . . . And did the rock say anything to you?'

Dad hesitated. 'Um, not in so many words . . . But I *sense* what it means. So I have to get back there fast to get back to work.'

Alfie cast a searching glance at Grandpa Werewolf, who was now leaning on his walking stick with his eyes closed. Mum moved in front of Dad and planted her hands on her hips.

'I don't think so, William Friend. I don't mind you hacking away at rocks. You can do that as much as you like. And you can have nice conversations with them too. That's fine by me. But I'm not having any rocks deciding when it's time for you to have a shower. That's my job. And I'm telling you now that you're going to have a shower first. And after that, you get a great big sandwich. Understood?' Mum stared Dad in the eye, unyielding, as if she was a rock too.

'OK,' Dad mumbled. 'A quick shower won't hurt. But then I'm off again, all right. I have to finish my statue today, before the full moon. I promised.'

Alfie suddenly noticed that Grandpa Werewolf was nodding, almost imperceptibly, as if he believed what Dad was saying. Or maybe it just looked like it, thought Alfie. He walked up to Dad.

'Can we have a quick look in the tent when you go back?'

'Yes,' said Tim, 'we're very curious about your work of art.'

Dad stared at Tim and Alfie with strange, fierce eyes that grew big and white in his black face.

'No! Nobody gets to see my sculpture

90

until it's finished. That's bad luck! And it's not finished yet, so that tent is off limits!' He wagged his finger at them, then turned and shuffled into the cottage, mumbling to himself.

Alfie looked at Noura and Noura looked at Tim. Tim winked.

21

'Ahem!'

'So, here we are,' Alfie whispered.

'I can see that,' Tim whispered back.

'What are we whispering for?' Noura whispered. 'There's no one here who can hear us. Your dad's miles away having a shower.'

After Mum and Dad had gone inside, they'd sneaked off. Leo and Grandpa Werewolf were hungry and had gone in too. Not having a chance to ask Grandpa any more questions, Alfie had slipped off quickly with Tim and Noura. And now they were standing in front of the tent.

It had grown overcast. Dark clouds drifted overhead and the wind was growing stronger, but Alfie didn't pay any attention. He was too busy gazing at Dad's tent. There were still signs everywhere.

```
GO AWAY!
TURN BACK!
NO UNAUTHORIZED ENTRY!
```

'The unauthorized again,' said Alfie. 'They're not allowed anywhere.'

There were even more signs than before.

```
GET LOST!
NO PEEPING!
TRESPASSERS WILL BE VERY
PROSECUTED!
```

Alfie sniggered.

'Dad really wants to keep it top secret!'

Tim walked between the signs and knelt

down next to the tent. 'He won't succeed though. We're going to be the first ones to secretly admire his work of art.'

'I'm really curious,' said Alfie as Tim reached for the zip.

'Wait!' Noura cried, looking thoughtful. 'It's not really fair, Tim. Your dad doesn't want anyone to see the statue before it's finished. That's very important to him. If we look anyway, we'll be cheating him.'

Tim and Alfie shrugged.

'I don't want to cheat anyone,' Alfie said, 'but what if we just have a very quick look? With one eye shut or something? Would that be OK?'

Noura shook her head. 'It's still cheating.'

Alfie thought for a moment, then nodded. 'Noura's right, Tim. Dad would never cheat us, so . . .'

Tim sighed and stood up. 'OK! Fine. Let's go home.' He looked up at the sky, which was growing darker by the minute. 'If you ask me, there's a storm coming.'

Suddenly a big smile appeared on his face.

'I almost forgot! We've arranged to meet Olga later.'

As he spoke, a blush appeared on his cheeks.

'Yeah, fun!' Alfie said. 'Come on, let's hurry back.'

Tim was already walking away.

'Pfff, what's the rush?' said Noura. Alfie sniggered and was about to follow Tim, when a cough came from the tent. 'Ahem!'

Alfie was sure he'd heard it. He froze.

'Did you hear that, Noura? Someone coughed in the tent.'

'Really?' Noura said. 'How could your dad be back already? He would have had to have run all the way.'

'But who else could it be?' Alfie said. 'Unless . . . Maybe he climbed out the bathroom window without Mum knowing. He wanted to get back to his rock as fast as he could, remember?'

Noura looked at the tent.

'Maybe. Are you sure you heard something?'

'Yes, I really heard it.'

Tim was waiting.

'What are you doing there?' he called. 'We have to go.'

Again coughing came from inside the tent. Harder this time. 'Agh-ghemm!'

It was a rough grinding sound. Even Tim heard it and hurried back. He studied the tent.

'Is Dad back already?'

'It seems like it,' Alfie said.

'Shall we have a look after all? Just to be sure.'

A bright bolt of lightning cast a white glow over everything, as if someone was taking a photo. The light flashed right through the tent and was immediately followed by a thunderclap. For just a second a big shadow was visible on the material of the tent. It was like a bending figure with a pointy nose and a sharp chin. Alfie felt his heart miss a beat.

I know that shadow, he thought. At least . . .

'Who's that?' he whispered.

Tim shrugged.

'Maybe it was just the shadow of some *thing* . . . the stump of a tree?' Noura whispered.

'I don't see any stumps anywhere,' said Alfie.

The next bolt of lightning and roar of thunder made them jump. The shadow on the tent was gone and the first drops of rain started to fall. Just then two figures appeared on the path, coming towards them. Growling and puffing.

22

No Body . . .

Alfie gaped at the approaching figures. A dark thundercloud was hanging over them. Grandpa Werewolf was holding up an umbrella and Leo was bounding around him like an enormous puppy.

Alfie burst out laughing. Leo hadn't changed into a werewolf yet because the full moon still hadn't risen – that would take a couple of hours – but he was already walking on all fours. He sniffed the trees and bushes and even stuck his nose into a molehill. The rain didn't seem to bother him at all.

'Hey, cuz wolf Alfie,' he yelled cheerfully. 'There youse be.'

'Hello, children,' Grandpa Werewolf panted, holding his hat and umbrella tight in the strong wind. They could hear rumbling in the distance, but the lightning had stopped.

'What are you doing here, Alfie? Not peeking into Tim's father's tent, I hope.' Grandpa Werewolf trained his fierce yellow eyes on Alfie, Tim and Noura in turn.

Alfie felt a blush appear on his face. 'Um, no, nothing like that, Grandpa Werewolf. Of course we didn't have a look. That's not allowed. It says so on the signs.'

Grandpa Werewolf nodded. 'Then hurry back to the cottage.'

The rain was getting heavier.

'Er, but we thought there was someone in the tent, Grandpa. We heard someone coughing.'

Grandpa Werewolf shook his head. A mysterious smile played over his lips.

'Don't worry, Alfie. Maybe someone coughed, but there's nobody in the tent. I know that for certain. Hurry off now! Otherwise you'll get drenched.'

Leo was nodding his head furiously. Drops of rain flew off his hair in all directions.

'Run like a greasy lightning rod, wolf cuz.

Run faster than a gravy hound. Other ways youse be wetter than a washing-up-liquid-brush.'

'Wow, Leo, you sound like a poet,' Alfie chuckled.

Leo nodded proudly. 'That be right, cuz! Leo be a super poemizer!'

Grandpa Werewolf raised an eyebrow at Alfie.

'OK, we're going, Grandpa.'

Tim and Noura ran off, but Alfie looked back one last time.

'Grandpa, shouldn't you and Leo go home too? You'll get sopping wet too, you know.'

Grandpa Werewolf shook his head. 'We'll take cover . . . somewhere.'

Alfie saw Grandpa Werewolf wink at Leo and Leo gave him a cross-eyed look in return.

'OK,' said Alfie, running after Tim and Noura. Grandpa Werewolf and Leo watched them go, Leo waving with his hands *and* his feet. They were standing under the umbrella and raindrops were bouncing off all around them. A strange idea popped into Alfie's head.

I think they're just waiting until we're gone, he thought. And then they're going to sneak into the tent to get out of the rain. But who was that shadow in the tent? He looked so familiar. It must have been Dad. Who else could it be?

He looked back one last time. Leo and Grandpa Werewolf had disappeared.

'Come on, Alfie!' Noura called.

Still trying to work it out, he ran after her and Tim. Just when they reached the cottage, the front door opened and Dad stepped out, scrubbed and cleaned and with a brand-new kangaroo tea cosy on his head.

'Hey,' Dad said with surprise. 'Where have you been?'

23

A Trollipop?

The full moon was high above the trees. Alfie and Noura had turned into werewolves and were running through the dark forest. Tim was trying to keep up with them.

'*Wrow*, I still don't understand,' said Alfie. 'Dad wasn't in the tent, but what was that shadow? I really thought—'

'It doesn't matter,' Tim said in a cheerful voice. 'We're going to meet up with Olga.'

'I hope she's there,' Alfie said. 'It'll be fun.'

'Really? Why do you think it will be

such good fun, Alfie?' Noura gave him a pointed look.

Alfie started to stutter. 'N-no reason. I, I . . . um, I just want to find out more about the werewolf orphanage. Don't you? You like O-olga too, don't you?'

'Maybe,' Noura said, a red glow flickering in her eyes. 'I don't know her that well, do I? You two act as if she's the nicest girl you know, but I want to find out what she's like first. Can we trust her?'

Alfie shook his head. 'You're the nicest girl I know, Noura. You know that.'

'Of course,' Tim said. 'You're the best, Noura . . . But I'd still like to get to know Olga a bit better. She's sweet. Don't you think, Alfie?'

Alfie looked at Noura out of the corner of his eye and saw her quickly turn her head. '*Wrow*, um, well . . . I think so. But, um, not necessarily.'

Noura didn't say a word.

They were getting close to the werewolf

orphanage. Alfie heard rustling in the bushes and had a funny feeling that something wasn't right.

'This is it,' Tim said. 'Where we agreed to meet. We were standing right next to this tree. What's the matter, Alfie?'

Alfie looked over his shoulder. 'I'm not sure. I think . . . I've got an idea we're being followed. Wait a sec, I'll just have a look.' He turned around and walked away from Tim and Noura.

'Come on, Alfie,' Noura called, but Alfie was already walking back down the path.

'*Wrow*, did I just see Grandpa Werewolf's shadow,' he growled to himself. 'Maybe he's here too?' He looked left and right and walked around a bush. 'It wouldn't surprise me,' he mumbled. 'I think Grandpa Werewolf is keeping something secret.' He stopped. Next to the shadow of a big tree there was a second shadow. A tall one with a big nose. Two big hairy feet were sticking out from behind the tree. They could only belong to one person, thought Alfie.

'*Wrow*, Leo! What are you doing here?'

A big werewolf's head poked out from behind the tree. It was Leo in his baggy overalls. He gave a crooked grin and waved cheerfully with a big black paw.

'Hi, cuz wolf. Leo has to peekaboos what youse be doing.'

'Who said so, Leo?'

'Grandpa Werewolfy.'

'Why?'

Leo shrugged. 'I don't nose, cuz wolf. I just sees and looks where youse be going.'

'And what are you and Grandpa going to do then, Leo?'

Leo scratched his head and peered down his nose. 'Then Leo goes with Grandpappa to get a trollipop, he thinks.'

'A trolley? What for? Is Grandpa planning something secret?'

Leo stared at the tip of his nose. A moth was sitting on it.

'Leo not be nosing that, cuz wolf. Maybe Grandpa Werewolfy all tired out and wants to sit in a trollipop to rest his old leggers?'

Leo was still peering at the insect on his nose.

'Leo don't nose nothing bout Grandpa's secret plannings.' He lashed out and brought his fist down on his nose. 'Ow!' Leo grabbed his nose with both hands and danced around in a circle. The moth fluttered off in the moonlight.

'Ow, ow, ow. Stupid buttery fly!'

Alfie burst out laughing. 'The poor little moth couldn't help it, Leo. It's just lucky to be alive. Hurry back to Grandpa Werewolf. Tell him we're at the werewolf orphanage. He'll know where it is.'

Leo nodded, his eyes crossed from the pain. 'Leo goes and tells. See youse later, cuz wolf.'

Shaking his head, Alfie watched Leo walk off into the trees.

'*Wrow*, a trolley! What do they want that for?'

Suddenly he heard a cry in the distance. Two cries! Alfie spun around and pricked up his ears. Tim and Noura . . .

24

Hush

What's that? thought Alfie. Are they calling me? Is Olga there already?

He hurried back. He could see Tim and Noura in the distance. There was someone else with them. Someone large and angular. What now?

Alfie dropped on to all fours and crept closer, hugging the ground and slinking from bush to bush. He peered at Tim and Noura. The other person obviously wasn't Olga. It was a fat, enormous werewolf instead.

The Big Box! Alfie realized. Mooma! He felt the shock through his whole body. She was wearing a dress and an apron, and glasses with very thick lenses. There were curlers in her hair.

Alfie heard her roaring voice. In the light of the moon her fangs glittered like shining daggers.

'So! A werewolf orphan running around loose with an accomplice. You thought you could make a monkey out of Mooma! That was a mistake. You're in for it now!' The big werewolf reached out and grabbed Tim and Noura by the scruffs of their necks. 'Oh, if only you knew how much Mooma loves her orphans.'

'I'm no orphan,' Noura growled. 'Let go, you horrible werewolf . . . lady.'

'Hush, quiet now, sweetie,' Mooma said gently. 'Orphan or not, you're coming with me.'

Her voice changed into a furious snarl.

'It's your own fault for coming here.'

'Ow,' Tim bellowed, 'my neck!'

Alfie had crept up behind a bush and was lying on his stomach. His heart was racing. He didn't get it: sometimes Mooma's voice sounded really mean, other times it was soft and gentle.

He watched the gigantic werewolf carry off Noura and Tim, who wriggled helplessly

in her arms. Noura made a strangled squeaking sound.

Behind the bush, Alfie groaned. He wanted to help, but Mooma was big enough to take on six werewolves at once. There was nothing he could do.

Mooma carried Tim and Noura up the hill to the house.

'Hush now, my darlings. I won't leave you behind. You're going to the icy cellar. To shiver with the others . . .'

25

Mooma Howls

Alfie crept on all fours, following Mooma as she stomped up the hill, a dark silhouette with the full moon behind her. Frogs leapt out of the way of her feet. Bats fluttered up and fled squeaking. Tim and Noura were clamped under her arms like two loaves of French bread.

Alfie saw Tim's feet kicking and heard Noura growling and spluttering. The big werewolf ignored them and walked up the stone staircase of the werewolf orphanage. At the top, in front of the door, Mooma turned. Her daunting head moved from left to right. Alfie saw a yellow glow in her eyes and for a second he was afraid that Mooma was looking for him. He hugged the ground.

Then Mooma raised her head in the air, looked at the full moon and let out a bloodcurdling howl. A howl that was mixed with a sob.

Alfie shuddered, pressed his front paws over his ears and buried his muzzle in the grass. It was the most terrifying werewolf howl he had ever heard. It sounded so terribly sad.

Almost as sad as I felt when I touched the weeping stone, thought Alfie. How is that possible?

WHAM!

Alfie jumped and looked up. The door to the werewolf orphanage was shut. Mooma had disappeared into the house with Tim and Noura.

What now? Alfie panicked. What do I do?

Slowly he sneaked up the stone steps and tiptoed over to the door, where he carefully raised the flap of the letterbox. He peered in through the narrow opening. The long hall was in front of him, with the walls and floor lit up by the light of the moon. At the end of the hall he saw Mooma disappear with Tim and Noura.

Am I brave enough to go inside? thought Alfie, wavering. No, I'm not brave enough. But I have to! He swallowed, grabbed the doorknob and quietly opened the door.

26

The Icy Cellar

The moon was shining brightly through the windows. Cautiously, Alfie crept down the hall, past the door of the Secret Room. The people in the paintings glowered down at him.

Alfie stopped for a moment to look at the portraits. Only now did he notice that the men and women had pointy ears as well as bushy sideburns and hairy faces.

I didn't pay much attention last time, he thought. They look a lot hairier now.

Suddenly he figured it out. Of course!

They were portraits of werewolves! Very ancient werewolves, maybe even from hundreds of years ago.

Strange! thought Alfie. Have werewolves always lived here? He scratched his head. It doesn't matter, he thought. I have to find Tim and Noura.

On tiptoe, he ran down to the dark end of the hall, where Mooma had disappeared into the darkness with Tim and Noura. A curving staircase led downwards.

So I have to go down the stairs too, thought Alfie. He wasn't keen. Who knows what's waiting for me down there in the darkness, he thought, looking around. There was no one in sight. Just the eyes in the portraits following him.

Alfie swallowed, then cautiously started down the stairs, one foot at a time. With every step it grew colder and darker. At the bottom of the stairs there was a wooden door. Alfie pressed his ear against it and heard vague sounds on the other side. He couldn't make out any words.

Tim and Noura are behind this door, he thought. This must be Mooma's icy cellar! A freezing draught blew past his hairy feet. Gently he pushed the door slightly open. A wave of cold air rose up to meet him from the inky darkness. He took a quick step back. Are they down there? He hoped not.

Again he peered through the opening. Suddenly a light flared up. Alfie saw more steps, stone this time, leading further down. Standing at the bottom was Mooma. She'd lit a candle and the flame cast a circle of light around her. Her shadow on the rough stone wall was enormous.

Alfie held his breath as he looked down through the crack. He jumped when Mooma's voice suddenly boomed through the cellar. It was so loud that, for a moment, Alfie thought she was talking to him.

'Wake up, little orphans. Look. Mooma caught two busybodies. They can keep you company in the icy cellar.'

The scruffy werewolf orphans were sitting in the circle of light. By the looks of them,

they'd been sitting in the dark for a long time. They rubbed their eyes and blinked at the unexpected glare.

Alfie made out the hairy faces of Igor, Olga and the other orphans. They were all shivering. Where's Noura, he thought. And Tim? He squinted, peered hard and finally spotted them, lying on the floor at Mooma's hairy feet. The reflected candlelight glinted in their frightened eyes.

Then one of the orphans stood up.

'M-m-may I p-p-please leave the c-c-cellar now, Mooma?'

Olga! thought Alfie. That's Olga's voice. He could see her trembling.

'I l-l-lured them here for you. M-may I go?'

Alfie couldn't believe his ears. Olga had lured them into a trap!

27

Betrayed

Stunned, Alfie peered at Olga through the crack. The candlelight danced over her muzzle and blonde werewolf fur. Alfie saw Tim and Noura staring at her in disbelief too.

Olga has betrayed us, thought Alfie. She pretended to be a friend. I thought she was sweet, but she's not! What a nasty, sickening trick! Noura was right. We shouldn't have trusted her.

'M-may I l-leave now?' Olga asked again. Alfie saw Mooma bend over her.

'Leave the icy cellar? You? Forget it,' she snarled. 'Sit! You stay here, just like the rest. Is that all right, dear little orphan girl?'

Shivering, Olga sat back down on the stone floor. The other werewolves didn't say a word. They seemed numb from the cold . . . or fear. Mooma's voice echoed through the cellar.

'No one's leaving this cellar. Ever again. We'll turn to stone here together.' There was a sob in her voice and she sniffed loudly. She sat down on the bottom steps of the stone staircase. 'Mooma's doing this for your own good, dear little orphans,' she said in a voice that was suddenly kind and gentle. 'You do understand that, don't you?'

Alfie saw the orphaned werewolves looking at each other.

'Um, are you going to start being nice again, like in the old days?' asked Igor.

Mooma shook her head. 'Nice? Mooma has to be hard as nails to protect you poor orphans from the cruel world, so you don't suffer like Mooma. Mooma's heart feels cold and lonely with a great sorrow locked up inside. A forgotten sorrow that hurts and burns like ice-cold fire.'

Mad, thought Alfie. This werewolf is completely bonkers! His heart was pounding. What do I do now? If only I could ask Tim for advice. And . . . Suddenly he heard Noura's voice.

'Please, Mrs Mooma, can Tim leave? He's not a werewolf like us . . .'

Alfie felt a lump in his throat.

Wow, Noura is so brave, he thought. She really is the best!

'What's that got to do with anything?' Mooma snarled. 'The human child stays here with us. He could betray us! No . . . no one is leaving! You will all stay here for ever!'

Again he heard Noura's voice.

'For ever? What do you mean by that, Mrs Mooma?'

For a second it stayed deathly quiet. Alfie could hear the silence rustling. Then Mooma answered with a sob.

'For ever. So that the cruel world can't hurt us ever again.' Mooma blew out the candle, plunging them into immediate darkness. Alfie jumped when he suddenly heard Mooma's footsteps stomping up the staircase.

She was already at the door . . .

28

Panic

Alfie spun around. Sweat was running past his hairy ears and down his neck.

Out of here! he thought. He could already hear Mooma's snorting and snuffling. He ran up the stairs as fast as he could and into the hall. He could see the front door in the distance, but it suddenly seemed a very long way away.

I won't make it, thought Alfie. Oh no, what do I do now? He could hear Mooma's footsteps on the stairs. He heard her growling and puffing. In a panic, Alfie looked around. The werewolves in the paintings seemed to have mocking smiles on their faces. A glow was burning in their eyes. Between the paintings was the door of the WSO Secret Room.

Alfie looked back. One of Mooma's paws appeared around the corner. No time to think. Into the room it was! Alfie pushed the door open and slipped inside.

The room looked just like it had the previous evening. The curtains in front of the tall windows were open and the moon was shining in. Quickly, Alfie closed the door behind him, waiting and listening. He couldn't hear any noise on the other side of the door. Was Mooma still there? Or had she moved on? Alfie was too scared to open the door to check.

He looked at the paintings. They were all portraits of werewolves. The wall opposite him didn't have any paintings on it. It was the wall with the trees.

'*Wrow!* They're the pedi-trees Noura was talking about. With names and photos and . . .' Alfie gasped. Written on one of the trees was his name: Alfie Span. And next to it was a photo. A photo of him . . .

29

A Fanlight

Alfie walked up to the wall and stared at the tree, touching the photo with one claw.

That . . . that's me! he thought. An ordinary photo of me as a boy. What's going on? How do they know my name? Where'd they get that photo?

His eyes glided over the tree. The name Alfred Spanman was written on the trunk and there were lots of other names on the branches: Paul Spanman, Stephanie Buckler, Elizabeth Spanman, Jerome Brewster, Ricardo Spanman. And it went on like that.

Some of the names didn't have a photo next to them.

They must be really old, thought Alfie. At least fifty years or so. From the days before photos were invented, I guess.

On the outside branch, Spanman changed into Span. Alfie stared at it disbelievingly.

Are all these people related to me? he wondered. My great-great-great-grandfathers and mothers? He scratched his head.

'*Wrow*, I've never heard of them. Is Grandpa Werewolf here too somewhere?'

There was a photo of a young man with a hat, but he was called Grimbeard. And there was a photo of someone called Ludwig Span.

I don't know either of them, thought Alfie.

Next to the photo of the young man with the hat there was a small portrait of a young woman. She looked sweet, with flowers in her hair.

I don't know her either, thought Alfie,

bending forward to read her name.

Suddenly there was a noise in the hall. Alfie turned back to the door in fright, bumping a chair and knocking it over with a bang. The footsteps stopped at the door.

Sugar! thought Alfie. Mooma! *Wro-oh!* She must have heard me.

His eyes flashed around the room. There was only one way out. One of the fanlights was open, but it was way up above the tall window. Much too high ... for an ordinary boy.

But not for a werewolf, thought Alfie. I can climb like a, um ... monkey. I think.

But there was no time left to think. The door was already opening. Alfie dug his claws into the red velvet curtain and quickly pulled himself up. *Rish, rish, rish.* His claws ripped into the fabric, but three seconds later he reached the fanlight and dived through it.

Landing in front of the window, he saw Mooma in the room, staring at the knocked-over chair. He caught a glimpse of her turning her head towards the window, then he was on the ground and pressing himself up against the wall.

Did she see me? he thought. He peered up past the window ledge and saw Mooma appear at the window. He lay there quiet as a mouse.

If she looks down, he thought, she'll see me, but Mooma didn't look down. She looked up at the full moon. Tears gleamed on her hairy cheeks. Her fierce wolf's howl could be heard through the glass. Alfie shivered and screwed up his eyes.

Why is she howling? From anger? Or from sorrow? He didn't dare move. Mooma could discover him at any moment. Alfie waited . . . and waited.

Suddenly there was a strange sliding noise. Followed by loud rattling. Alfie couldn't hold back any longer, he crept forward and looked up.

The window was no longer visible. It was now covered by heavy metal shutters.

Oh, no, she's closing up the house,

thought Alfie. Sealing it off. Nobody will be able to get out any more! Not Tim and not Noura either. He leapt up and ran off without looking back. He could only think of one thing.

30

The Dentmobile

I have to get help! Alfie thought, racing through the forest as fast as he could go. Trees whizzed past. His feet slid over rocks, grass and branches. Above his head, the full moon floated along behind him. And meanwhile the song wind reached his ears:

> *A vampire too can feel the pain*
> *In a stony heart that beats no more*
> *But if he sees his love again*
> *That heart will beat just like before*

'*Wrow*, go away, wind, with your stupid songs,' Alfie growled. 'I don't want to listen to you. I have to get help for Tim and Noura before it's too late.' He ran along the bank of Silver River, which was babbling quietly in the moonlight. He could already see Dad's tent. Alfie ran around it.

'Dad, Dad, help!' he shouted. 'We have to . . .' He fell silent in astonishment.

Tim's father was sitting on the ground in front of the tent with a hammer and chisel between his feet. The kangaroo tea cosy was crooked on his head and he was staring into space with a miserable expression on his face.

'*Wrow*, Dad, what are you doing?' Alfie asked. 'We have to . . .'

Dad looked up. His eyes were glazed over.

'I just had to do a pee, Alfie,' he said. 'So I stepped out of the tent. Just for a minute or two. To look for a nice pee tree. And when I came back he was gone.'

Alfie scratched his head with surprise.

'*Wrow*, what do you mean? Who was gone? We don't have time for—'

Dad sighed deeply. 'My statue. The beautiful statue I hacked out of that rock with my hammer and my chisel, with grit, sweat and tears. It walked off. The ungrateful lump of rock. Look for yourself. The tent is empty.'

'That's impossible, Dad. Statues can't walk.'

Dad sighed again. 'No? Where's he gone then?'

Alfie shrugged impatiently. '*Wrow*, I don't know, Dad. Maybe someone stole the statue. But now you have to come with me. Tim and Noura are in danger.'

'What?' Dad shook his head. He seemed to be slowly waking up from a dream. 'Tim and Noura in danger? How? Where are they?'

Quickly, Alfie explained what had happened.

'Wow,' Dad said, staring into space. 'A house full of orphaned werewolves!

That's super cool.'

'*Wrow*, not at all,' Alfie growled. 'Tim and Noura are being held prisoner in that house.'

That got through to Dad. He jumped up. 'Then we have no time to lose, Alfie. Show me the way. We'll go and free Tim and Noura first, and then we'll look for my statue.' Dad straightened the kangaroo tea cosy, picked up his hammer and chisel and stuck them in his belt. 'I'll hack that house open if I have to! It can't be that difficult. It will be like opening a big tin of baked beans.'

'Um, maybe we need more help,' Alfie growled. 'Shall we go and get Leo and Grandpa Werewolf?'

Just then they heard the roar of an engine. Branches broke, bushes bent aside, birds screeched and took off from the trees. A double beam of light swept over Dad and Alfie and swiped the tent. Two bright headlights approached through the darkness. Brakes screeched and sand went flying.

Dad and Alfie leapt out of the way in the nick of time. With a bang, the car flattened Dad's tent and sent the No Entry signs flying in all directions before stopping with a dull thud. The door opened and Mum climbed out.

'Spit it out! What's happening?'

31

Upside Down

Dad and Alfie were struck dumb. They looked at Mum, then stared at the flattened tent and the scattered signs.

'Sorry about your tent, dear, but there's something wrong. As a mother, I sensed that. That's why I came here as fast as I could. Well, also partly because Grandpa Werewolf warned me this afternoon. "It's going to happen tonight," he said.'

Grandpa Werewolf *does* know something! thought Alfie. Something we don't. Maybe that's why he sent us here in the first place.

'Sweetheart,' Dad said. 'You are absolutely right, as always. It's a disaster, my beautiful rock is gone and—'

Mum held up a hand to stop him. 'That's not what I mean, William. Where are Tim and Noura?'

'Oh,' Dad said. 'Of course, that's more important. Don't be frightened, it's nothing very terrible. A lunatic lady werewolf has got diabolical plans for them.'

Alfie nodded. '*Wrow*, they're locked up in that big house on the hill.'

'But I'm going to open it with my tin

opener,' Dad explained. 'Um, I mean my hammer and chisel.'

Mum didn't flinch. 'Come on, get in.'

'Where are Leo and Grandpa Werewolf?' Alfie asked.

'No idea,' Mum said. 'They left a while ago. To get some kind of trolley or something. Either way, I haven't seen them since.'

'What on earth do they need a trolley for?' Alfie asked.

'No idea, son. They were acting a little mysterious.' Mum smiled. 'But, of course, werewolves are always mysterious at full moon. You know all about that, Alfie.' She got into the car and started the engine.

'Wait a sec,' Dad said. 'You can't actually drive through this forest. There aren't any roads, just narrow paths and lots of trees. And there are hidden chasms. Plus we have to go up a steep hill. You can't do that in a car.'

Mum gripped the steering wheel and winked. 'Want to bet? They didn't take away my driving licence for nothing.'

'What?' Dad cried. 'Again? When?'

'Today!' Mum beamed. 'Get in and put on your seat belts!'

Alfie jumped into the back seat and the Dentmobile shot forward with a growl, sending sand and dust flying up around the windows.

Alfie filled in Mum on the way. That wasn't easy with the car jolting and jerking down the path. Alfie bounced up and down on the back seat like a tennis ball and felt like he was in a runaway dodgem car. Fortunately the seat belt was holding him in place.

Mum listened silently to Alfie. The beams of the headlights zigzagged over the undergrowth like searchlights and the trees seemed to step out of the way in fright.

We can't keep being lucky, thought Alfie. He noticed that Dad had pulled the kangaroo hat down over his eyes. Skidding and sliding from side to side, the car worked its way up the hill. It was a mystery how

Mum kept it going.

'Are we almost there, dear?' Dad asked from under the kangaroo.

A big tree suddenly loomed up in front of the car, its branches spread like giant arms. Alfie screwed up his eyes and held his breath. The brakes screeched like seagulls. The car seemed to buck, then took off into the air. Alfie felt it tipping. His stomach shot up into his throat and his head banged against the roof.

Then, suddenly, they were motionless.

For a moment no one spoke. The engine had fallen silent too. Alfie felt like his ears were lying flat against his head from terror. The roof of the car was pressing against his head. How could it do that?

Mum spoke first.

'Here we are. Is this the house?'

Carefully Alfie opened his eyes. He saw that Tim's mother and father were just as shocked as he was. They too were sitting straight with their heads pressed against the roof of the car. Dad's kangaroo hat was squashed and Mum's shoulder bag was lying on the ceiling.

Very strange! thought Alfie.

He looked out of the front window and, for a moment, didn't understand what he was seeing.

It was incredible! They were right outside the werewolf orphanage. But there was something funny about it. The house was upside down.

32

Tree Root

Alfie stared at the werewolf orphanage with astonishment. What's going on? he thought. Who turned the house upside down? And what's the moon doing under it? That's impossible!

It took a while for him to work it out. It wasn't the house that was upside down, it was the Dentmobile! So I must be upside down too, thought Alfie. That's why the roof is pressing against my head so hard! And the seat belt's the only thing keeping me in place. I'm like a werewolf

on a flying trapeze.

Mum and Dad were hanging upside down in their seat belts too.

'Nice driving, dear,' Dad squeaked with the seat belt against his throat. 'You made it to the top of the hill without hitting a single tree. Now we just need to get out of the car.'

'Easy,' Mum replied, opening the door, unclicking the seat belt and tumbling sideways out of the car. Alfie slipped out of his belt too and did a forward roll to get out of the car.

'Help me will you, please, sweethearts,' Dad called. 'I'm stuck and the blood is slowly running to my head.'

Chuckling, Mum and Alfie helped him out of the car. He stood up immediately and put the squashed kangaroo back on his head.

'There, right as rain.' He wobbled and almost fell over. Mum and Alfie grabbed hold of him.

'Whoops,' he said. 'I'm a little dizzy. It must be from all that hacking away at my statue. A true artist always keeps going till he drops. Grandpa Werewolf said so too. 'Keep hacking,' he said. 'Then something will emerge of its own accord.'

Strange, thought Alfie. Behind the scenes, Grandpa Werewolf has been doing a lot of talking. As if he has a secret plan.

He looked at the Dentmobile. The car was lying helplessly on its back like a flipped turtle. The wheels were spinning in the air.

Behind the car was the massive, dark werewolf orphanage, without a light showing anywhere. Metal shutters had been lowered in front of the door and all the windows.

'So Tim and Noura are being held captive in that house by a mad lady werewolf?' Mum asked.

Alfie nodded. 'In the icy cellar.'

'We have to get in,' Mum said.

'*Wrow*, but how? It's sealed off completely with metal shutters!'

Dad pulled a hammer and chisel out of his belt like a cowboy pulling two revolvers out of his holsters.

'Leave it to me. My dizzy fit has already passed.'

Suddenly Alfie remembered something. '*Wrow*, wait a minute. Olga said that there was a secret entrance to the cellar. If we can find that, we can—'

Dad wasn't listening. He strode up to the front door, set the chisel on the metal shutter and swung the hammer. CLANG!

146

It didn't leave a scratch on the shutter, but the hammer bounced back and hit Dad on the forehead.

'Ow!' he roared. The chisel flew out of his hand and landed on his foot.

'Ouch-ouch-ouch!' Dad hopped around, holding his forehead with both hands.

'Watch out, dear,' Mum called. 'There's a . . .'

Dad's hopping foot got caught on something.

'Prickle bush.'

Dad toppled forward. 'Eek!'

Mum and Alfie hurried over to him and helped him out of the bush.

'Poor dear,' Mum said, anxiously studying the prickles in Dad's arms, legs and face. 'You suddenly look very . . . prickly.'

Dad nodded. His voice sounded weak. 'I feel a bit like a cactus.'

Mum very carefully pulled a prickle out of Dad's eyebrow.

'Ou-wah!'

Alfie felt sorry for Dad and looked down

at the root he'd tripped over. Hey, he thought. That looks like . . . He bent down and touched the root. Iron! It was an iron handle, sticking up out of the grass. Quickly Alfie scraped away the grass and soil with his claws, uncovering a square wooden lid.

'*Wrow*, Dad, Mum, look at this, quick,' Alfie panted. 'I've found something . . .'

33

Secret Passage

'What is it, Alfie?'

Mum hurried over with Dad hobbling along behind her, whimpering as he pulled prickles out of his arms and legs. Alfie pointed at the lid.

'*Wrow*, there's something under this thing here.' Alfie grabbed the handle and pulled. The lid swung up as if it was weightless and the moon lit up an opening in the ground.

A-ha, this was how Olga was able to get out so easily, thought Alfie. And back in again.

'Look. This must be the secret passage to the cellar.'

Mum peered into the inky depths. 'Are you sure, Alfie? It looks very narrow. I'm not sure anyone could fit through there.'

Alfie bent over the opening and felt cold air on his face. 'Maybe not *anyone*, but a little werewolf can. Olga crawled through too.'

Mum looked at him anxiously. 'Are you sure it's a good idea, son? That passage looks scary.'

'Yes,' Dad said. 'What if you get stuck? Or come out on the other side of the world. In China or somewhere like that. How would we ever get you back? I don't know my way around China.'

Alfie swallowed. He knew that Tim's mum and dad loved him a lot. Just as much as they loved Tim.

'*Wrow*, I have to, Mum. Tim and Noura are down there with that crazy werewolf. There's no time to lose.'

Mum gave a deep sigh and rummaged through her shoulder bag. 'You don't know where it leads, Alfie. At least take this with you.' She handed Alfie a thin torch.

'Wait, wait,' Dad cried. He picked a prickle out of his lower lip. 'Ow!' Then he pulled a penknife out of his tool belt. 'Here, Alfie. You might need this.'

Alfie gaped at the knife. '*Wrow*. Do you want me to . . . um . . . stab Mooma, Dad?'

'No, of course not. But a penknife might come in handy. You never know. It's got manicure scissors and everything.'

Alfie nodded hesitantly. '*Wrow*, I don't think I'll have time to cut my nails in the passage, Dad, but thanks.' He put the penknife in his pocket. 'I'll be off then.'

'You be careful, Alfie,' Mum said. 'We'll wait here for you.'

Armed with the torch, Alfie crawled into the passage.

34

A Wereworm

Alfie wriggled down the narrow tunnel on his stomach with the torch clamped between his teeth. A small circle of light slid down in front of him. In his thoughts Alfie saw himself slithering forward. He heard noises that only werewolves can hear. The rustling, scampering and scuttling of little insect feet.

I'm just like a worm, he thought. A wereworm. He struggled on down the tunnel, which seemed to go on for ever. Suddenly a terrible thought occurred to

him. What if this tunnel really does come out somewhere completely different? Maybe it goes right under the forest. Under all those trees, rocks and bushes. Maybe it does come out in another country. Or in the sea! Then I'll get lost or drown or go on for ever. And I'll never see Tim and Noura again . . .

Beads of sweat stung his neck. His eyes were watering. He got a queasy feeling in his stomach.

'Don't panic, Alfie,' he whispered. 'You're no wimp. You're a ferocious werewolf. You

can't go back because you can't turn around.
The tunnel is way too narrow. You have to
go on.'

'Hey, Alfie! Are you OK?'

Mum's voice sounded very far away, but
he could understand her perfectly.

'*Wrow*, yes, sure!' he shouted at the top of
his voice. 'It's going fine, Mum!'

'Good. Don't give up, son!' Dad boomed.
'At least you're dry in there. Out here it's
starting to rain.'

Alfie giggled and sighed with relief. All of
a sudden he wasn't scared any more.

Did Grandpa Werewolf know about this
tunnel? he wondered. Maybe Grandpa
even crept through here once when he was
a young werewolf. He had to laugh at the
idea of Grandpa as a little werewolf with a
hat and a walking stick.

He crawled on further until the tunnel
suddenly stopped at a stone wall. There was
a hole in it, just big enough for a young
werewolf. He shone his torch through it.

From somewhere in the darkness he

heard loud snoring. He also heard a strange clicking sound: *click-click-click, clack-clack-clack* . . .

He shone the torch around, tracking the beam over the floor of a big room. The freezing icy cellar, he thought. Suddenly the light flickered. Oh, no! Surely the batteries aren't finished? Alfie shook the torch and the light flicked back on.

Alfie aimed the torch at the ceiling and then at the walls. The cellar was a cave full of black shadows. Spiders crept over the walls. A bat somersaulted through the beam of light.

Alfie moved the torchlight to the middle of the cellar and all at once eight pairs of blinking eyes were staring at him. The strange clicking noise was even louder now. *Clack-clack-clack, click-click-click* . . .

35

Cutting the Rope

Alfie almost dropped the torch from shock. He could suddenly see everything very clearly, as if he was looking at a big photo. In the middle of the cellar there was a long couch, with Mooma lying back on it on big colourful cushions. She was snoring like three bears.

'Grrrrrr . . . ppyyooo, grrrr . . . ppyyooo . . .'

Sitting around the couch were the orphan werewolves, Tim and Noura. They blinked and stared anxiously at the torchlight. They looked dazed and drowsy and their teeth were chattering. *Click-click-click, clack-clack-clack*. Tim and Noura were shivering.

Again the torch flickered.

Uh-oh, I'd better hurry up, thought Alfie. The batteries really are running out. Quickly he crawled through the hole and into the cellar, where he immediately felt the cold rising up from his feet to his legs. No wonder the orphans' teeth are chattering like that, he thought.

He tiptoed closer, then held an index finger up to his lips. 'Shhh!'

They looked at him but didn't say a word.

'Psst, Noura, Tim,' Alfie whispered. 'I've come to rescue you.' He shone the torch on his face for a second. '*Wrow*, look . . . It's me.'

'Alfie!' Noura whispered. 'I couldn't see who it was.'

'Great,' Tim said softly. 'But we can't get away. We're all tied to Mooma.'

Alfie saw ropes around their necks. The ropes were tied to Mooma's wrists and ankles.

Smart of the old werewolf! thought Alfie.

'The orphans can't move a muscle,' Noura said. 'And neither can we. If we move, we'll wake up Mooma.'

Alfie pulled the penknife out of his pocket and opened it. 'Lucky for us I've got a penknife. Good thinking from Dad.' For a second Alfie aimed the torch at Mooma. Her big werewolf head was leaning back against the backrest. She was still sound asleep. Her massive chest rose up with every snore, then she blew her breath back out with a whistling sound.

'Grrrr . . . ppyyooo, grrrr . . . ppyyooo . . .'

'*Wrow*, the kettle's boiling.' Quickly he aimed the torch back at the floor.

'Hurry, Alfie,' Noura whispered. 'Cut us loose before Mooma wakes up.'

Alfie nodded. Very carefully he started to cut the rope connecting Noura and Mooma. It wasn't easy. The rope was thick and his hairy paw was shaking.

'I-I'm not that good with a knife,' he growled softly.

'Relax,' Noura whispered. 'You'll manage.'

Alfie felt the sweat running down his neck and sighed. He was almost through the rope. There was just one thin thread left. Suddenly Mooma groaned in her sleep and moved her head. Her eyes opened and stared at Alfie. Alfie was so frightened he growled at the top of his voice.

'*WROW!*'

36

WROW!

'I can't see a thing down that hole!' Dad lay on his stomach and peered into the dark tunnel with one eye. 'No, nothing at all,' he said. 'And I can't hear anything either.'

The rain was getting heavier and heavier. Mum pulled an umbrella out of her shoulder bag and looked at her watch impatiently.

'What's keeping our boys now? It's already ten minutes since Alfie crawled into that hole.'

Dad scrambled back up on to his feet. 'Relax, sweetheart. Give them some time.'

Mum nodded, opening the umbrella. 'You're right. But I don't want anything to happen to them. And not to Noura either, of course.' She looked up at the full moon. 'And where have Leo and Grandpa Werewolf got to? They've been gone for a very long time. Why are they looking for a trolley?'

Dad shrugged. 'It's full moon and you know how that affects werewolves. They do things ordinary people like us just don't understand. Things we can only dream of . . .' He sighed deeply. 'Oh, if only I could change into a werewolf just once! That would be so super cool. That's *really* different.'

Mum smiled. 'Dear, how often have I told you? As far as I'm concerned, you don't need to be a werewolf at all. So stop complaining. Otherwise I'll box your ears.'

Dad raised his hands to protect himself. 'OK, I won't say another word.'

He looked up at the black rain clouds with a worried expression.

'I wonder where my beautiful statue is.

Maybe it's wandering aimlessly and alone through the rain. Or maybe thieves have stolen it and it's lying in the back of a lorry somewhere.' He sighed again and pulled a prickle out of his chin. 'All that work in vain. All my hacking, all my grit, sweat and tears for nothing.'

Just then there was a loud growl, far away in the underground tunnel.

'WROW!'

37

Anger

Horrified and too scared to move, Alfie looked straight into Mooma's big yellow eyes.

It's over, he thought. Stupid, stupid, stupid! I've blown it now. Mooma will get me too. We've all had it . . .

It seemed like Mooma was staring at him for minutes. Then her eyelids drooped and she started snoring again. It had only been a couple of seconds.

Alfie couldn't believe it. That was close!

It gave him new strength. With one slash

he cut through the last bit of rope. Noura was free. Then he cut Tim's rope easily.

'Quick, Noura, Tim, get out of here,' Alfie whispered.

Noura shook her head. 'First the orphans! They've been stuck here a lot longer and they're all frozen half to death.'

Alfie looked at Igor, who was sitting next to Tim with his teeth chattering.

'*Wrow*, OK.' He handed the torch to Tim. 'Can you give me some light, Tim?' Holding his knife, Alfie bent over Igor, who looked at him with big eyes.

'Don't be scared,' Alfie whispered. He cut the rope and helped Igor up. Mooma was still snoring as loud as ever.

'Quick, to the opening,' Alfie whispered.

'Th-thanks,' Igor growled, still shivering. Tim lit the way with the torch and Igor climbed out through the hole.

'*Wrow*, perfect,' Alfie growled. 'Now the others.' He carefully cut Inouk's rope then Ashanti's. '*Wrow*, it's going well,' he growled softly. 'I'm cutting as well as a . . . um, butcher.' One after the other he sent the orphans over to the opening until finally there was just one left: Olga. She alone was still tied to Mooma's thick, hairy ankle. The others had all crawled up the tunnel.

Tim and Noura were waiting. Looking at Olga, Alfie felt anger in his stomach. It's all because of her, he thought. Otherwise we'd be happy and free now, running around under the full moon. He was sure that his eyes were turning a deep red.

'*Wrow*, Olga. You betrayed Noura. And Tim and me too. That wasn't very nice of you.'

Olga looked at him desperately. 'Please cut me free too, Alfie. I'm so sorry. I . . . I didn't want to betray you. But I was so scared . . . of the icy cellar. Of having to stay here for ever.'

Tears rolled down over her muzzle. The torch flickered again in Tim's shaking hand. The light was a lot weaker now.

'Alfie, hurry up,' Noura whispered. 'Cut her loose, fast. She's sorry.'

Alfie looked up and tried to pull himself together. For a moment he was shocked by his werewolf rage. He hadn't known he could feel so furious. Slowly the red haze in front of his eyes faded. Quickly he cut Olga's rope.

'Hurry up, Olga, get out of here.'

Olga jumped up and ran to the opening. After she'd disappeared, Noura crawled into the hole.

'Come quickly, Tim, Alfie,' she said quietly.

Alfie looked at Mooma, who was still snoring away, the cut ropes dangling from her wrists and ankles.

'You first, Tim. Then me.'

Tim nodded, handing the torch back to Alfie.

'Don't dawdle, huh, Alfie?'

'*Wrow*, go on.'

Quickly Tim crawled into the hole. Alfie saw him disappear in the faint light of the torch. Then he couldn't see anything any more. The torch had gone out for good now and it was pitch black. He noticed something funny too. The snoring had stopped.

It was quiet in the cellar. Dead quiet and very dark. He searched for the opening in the wall. Fortunately his werewolf eyes adjusted to darkness quickly and he could soon make things out. The entrance to the narrow tunnel was right in front of him. He stretched out an arm.

Suddenly he heard a shuffling sound behind him. Then footsteps: *Stomp, stomp.* Alfie's hair stood on end. A flickering light cast shadows on the wall. Slowly he turned around.

38

Found?

Mum and Dad were outside waiting at the
entrance to the secret tunnel. The full moon
was half hidden behind a black cloud that
was softly raining on Dad's kangaroo tea
cosy. Mum was sheltering under the
umbrella. Together they gaped as the young
werewolves crawled out of the hole, one
after the other, until they were all standing
shivering in the drizzle, six wet werewolves
huddled together. They seemed a little bit
scared of Mum and Dad. Dad pinched his
nose shut.

'Poo, they smell like wet dogs.'

'Don't be silly, dear,' Mum said. 'The poor wet . . . um, werewolf children. Come here under my umbrella. This rain keeps getting heavier.' She pulled four of the sopping-wet orphans towards her. Dad took off his kangaroo.

'The others can take cover under my tea cosy. I'll squeeze my nose shut. It's too bad the car's upside down, otherwise we could get into that.'

The other two orphans looked at him anxiously, shrugged, growled something under their breath and shook their heads.

'You don't have to if you don't want to. It's up to you, you know.' Dad let go of his nose and put the tea cosy back on his head. Meanwhile Noura had climbed out of the hole with Tim just behind her.

'Hi, Mum. Hi, Dad,' he called.

'Hooray, there they are!' Mum shouted. 'You're saved. Alfie's done really well.'

Dad nodded. 'Fantastic! But where is our hero?'

Tim wiped the rain out of his eyes. 'Alfie was going to follow behind us. What's keeping him?'

Bright white lightning flashed through the sky, followed by a loud clap of thunder.

'Uh-oh!' Mum looked up. Dark clouds had gathered overhead like a flock of black sheep, blocking out the moon almost completely.

'Now we're in for it,' she said as the rain started to pour down harder and harder.

Noura was kneeling at the secret entrance.

'Alfie!' she called. 'You coming?'

There was no answer. Alfie didn't appear.

Behind them they heard panting and a squeaking noise and everyone turned around. Leo and Grandpa Werewolf were just emerging from a curtain of rain on their way up the hill. Leo groaned. His overalls were sopping and rainwater was dripping from the legs. A thick rope ran over his shoulder to a wobbly trolley with squeaky wheels. Standing on the trolley

171

was a big black statue.

'This be one heavisome trollipop!'
Leo called. 'With a super-heavy lump
of rockstone.'

Dad jumped for joy and threw his
kangaroo tea cosy up in the air. 'My statue!
My dear beautiful statue. They've found
it!' Overcome by excitement, he jumped

up and down in a puddle of water. But then he suddenly stopped. 'Or . . . or did they *steal* it?'

Grandpa Werewolf waved his umbrella. 'Sorry, but we had to steal your statue, father of Tim. You would never have given it to us, but we need it.' Panting, he stopped in front of Mum and Dad. 'We're not too late, are we?' he growled.

There was another flash of lightning. Somewhere far behind the werewolf orphanage they heard a loud werewolf's howl.

'Woo-hoo-oooo!'

39

Mooma's Armpit

Mooma was standing in front of Alfie with a burning candle, her yellow eyes glowing in its light. She laid a paw on Alfie's shoulder and bent her big werewolf head close to his. Alfie got goosebumps all over. That seemed very strange for a werewolf, but he had no time to think about it.

'Who are you?' Mooma growled. 'Does Mooma know you from somewhere? You look familiar.'

Alfie held his jaw clenched shut.

'Where are Mooma's orphans?' Mooma demanded.

'U-um . . .' Alfie stammered. Mooma's paw was heavy on his shoulder. Her eyes went to the hole in the wall.

'Oh, Mooma understands.'

For a moment her eyes took on a look of intense sadness.

'You . . . you helped the werewolf orphans

to escape. You sent them back into the cruel world.' Mooma shook her head and Alfie saw tears gleaming in the corners of her eyes. 'Stupid of you, you poor werewolf cub. It's a shame. A terrible pity. You shouldn't have done it. They should have stayed here with me for ever. The werewolf orphans and Mooma. Away from all pain and sorrow. Now Mooma can't save them. You've ruined everything!'

With these last words, Mooma's voice turned mean and grating again. She took a deep breath and closed her eyes. She seemed to be pondering something. Alfie was too scared to speak. Her heavy paw was still pressing down on his shoulder.

Mooma opened her eyes and sighed deeply. Alfie saw a tear running down her werewolf cheek.

'Then we'll do it differently,' Mooma said. 'Mooma's not going to wait any more. You're the only orphan Mooma has left, so Mooma's going to save you, whether you want her to or not!'

'*Wrow*, I'm not an orphan. I've been adopted by—'

'Shut your trap, orphan or not!' Mooma grabbed Alfie and clamped him under her arm.

'*Wrow*, wait, please, Mrs Big Box, um . . . Mrs Mooma,' Alfie squeaked. It was hard to breathe squashed under Mooma's arm and the pong was something else.

'Where are we going?'

Mooma glared at him. 'We're on our way to the end . . .'

40

The Chasm

Alfie held his breath, trying to block out the smell of Mooma's armpit.

What is she doing? Where is she going? he thought.

Mooma walked up the stairs, bashed the door open and took the next staircase. Then she stormed down the hall to the kitchen. Like all the other doors and windows, the back door was covered by a roll-down metal shutter. Alfie saw Mooma press a button and the shutter rattled up. Mooma opened the back door and stepped out into the howling wind and splashing rain. Alfie looked around. They were at the back of the orphanage, somewhere he'd never been before.

A path with big rocks on either side led further up the hill. Black clouds swirled past the moon like frightened sheep. The rain clattered on the rocks. The wind blew through the trees.

Alfie caught snatches of the song wind's song.

Long, long ago Armando was young
In love with life, in love with blood . . .

Mooma just kept stomping up the hill. She mustn't hear the wind, thought Alfie as the rain spattered on his glasses.

'*Wrow*, Mrs Mooma, where are we going?' he called. 'What is the end?'

Mooma didn't answer. A lightning bolt lit up the surroundings with bright white light. Alfie saw the rocks and trees as a black-and-white photo. He tried to wriggle loose.

Mooma ignored the lightning and Alfie

too. She held him tight and pushed on against the storm.

This is all going wrong, thought Alfie. I don't want this to be the end!

He tried to squirm out of Mooma's grip but her arm was wrapped around him like a steel clamp. The trees were bent over in the blasting wind and the rain was pushing the bushes flat to the ground.

Nothing can stop Mooma, thought Alfie. Not even wind, rain and storm. What can I do now?

Finally Mooma reached the top, where the path stopped. Alfie looked up at Mooma anxiously. She raised her head in the air. The moon was half visible behind the black clouds.

'*Wrow*, what have we come here for?' Alfie asked, shivering. 'It's cold and wet and windy. You'll catch a cold here, you know! And so will I.'

Mooma held him in her arms like a baby and looked at him. Her eyes were watery. Or was that just the rain?

'We'll never catch anything again, little werewolf orphan. This is the end of everything.' She was silent for a moment, then growled, 'Plus you helped my poor orphans to escape. You have to suffer for that!'

Alfie gulped. 'W-where is this end, Mrs Mooma? Do you mean the end of the path?'

Mooma shook her head. 'Too late, poor werewolf orphan! Sweet little orphan.

Naughty, troublesome orphan. Look!'
Mooma held Alfie in front of her with
outstretched arms.

He looked down in fright and his stomach
turned. There was nothing under his feet,
just a black chasm. So deep he couldn't see
the bottom.

'Down there,' Mooma said. 'The end
of everything is down there. And that's
where we're going. You and Mooma . . . No
more sorrow.'

Tears poured down over her werewolf
cheeks. She opened her mouth wide
and howled at the full moon. 'Woo-
woo-wooooo!'

41

A Procession

It's going to happen now, thought Alfie. Mooma is going to leap into the chasm. And she's going to take me with her. I don't want to!

Alfie screwed up his eyes. In his thoughts he saw Tim, Noura, Mum and Dad's faces. Leo and Grandpa Werewolf flashed by too. He even heard Leo saying, 'Cuz wolf, what you be doing now?'

I'll never see them again, Alfie thought, before his fear grew too enormous. So big that it started to numb him.

I'm going to fall any second now, he thought with a smile. It's kind of funny! Then, from far away, he heard a familiar voice.

'Mooma!'

That . . . that's Grandpa Werewolf's voice, thought Alfie. Am I dreaming? He opened his eyes. I'm still alive, he thought. And I'm not dreaming!

Mooma turned around. In the distance Alfie saw a whole procession approaching with one figure after the other emerging from the falling rain. His heart leapt.

Grandpa Werewolf was leading the way, bent over under an umbrella. Leo, Tim and Noura were pulling a trolley on which a large black figure was standing. The orphans were pushing the trolley from behind and Mum and Dad were walking next to them.

'Mooma, don't do it!' Grandpa Werewolf called, waving his umbrella.

Alfie was still dangling over the chasm. He kicked desperately and held Mooma's arms tight.

'*Wrow*, please don't drop me, Mrs Mooma! I don't want to fall.'

Mooma looked at the approaching procession.

'Too late,' she said. 'Mooma has had enough.' She turned her back on them and shuffled forwards. Her big, hairy feet were already sticking out over the edge of the chasm.

'No!' Noura screamed.

'Mooma, don't do it!' Alfie heard Grandpa

Werewolf again, his voice even mightier this time. 'He's . . . your grandson!'

A bolt of lightning split the night, lighting up Grandpa's werewolf muzzle.

42

Armando

Huh? thought Alfie. What does Grandpa Werewolf mean?

'Huh?' said Tim.

'Huh?' said Mum and Dad.

'Really?' said Noura.

'Grimbeard!' Mooma said. 'Is that you? It's been a long time. A very long time!'

Alfie gripped Mooma's arms in terror. He saw the astonishment on Mooma's face as she looked back at Grandpa. She seemed to have forgotten all about Alfie.

Don't drop me! he thought.

Mooma smiled sadly. Her gleaming white fangs sparkled in the moonlight.

'You're lying, Grimbeard . . . Mooma has no grandson. Once . . . Yes, once there was a human child. But that's a very long time ago . . .' She shook her head furiously. 'No! That was just a dream, wasn't it?' Mooma brought one paw up to her head, sobbing quietly. 'Stop it, Grimbeard! Mooma has no one and nothing!'

Grimbeard? thought Alfie. Wasn't that the young man in the photo?

Grandpa Werewolf took off his hat. The rain ran down past his ears. It was the last drops. A gentle breeze was blowing away the thunderstorm. Grandpa Werewolf stared at Mooma and shook his head.

'That's not true, Mooma,' he said softly. 'You do have someone. I've brought him here for you. Someone you've had to do without for a very long time. Look . . .'

Leo pushed the trolley with the black statue closer. 'Look, here's Father Chiminny Christmas. Isn't he nice and shiny and

188

pitcherful black?'

'What?' said Mooma. 'Who . . .'

Just then the black clouds drifted apart, revealing the full moon. Bright beams of moonlight shone down on the wet, black statue, making it gleam and shine. Mooma froze and seemed to have turned into a statue herself. Softly the song wind sang its tune between the rocks:

> *A vampire too can feel the pain*
> *In a stony heart that beats no more*
> *But if he sees his love again*
> *That heart will beat just like before*

'Armando!' Mooma whispered.

43

Slippery

Alfie was still dangling over the chasm. He gripped Mooma's arms and looked up at her anxiously.

'*Wrow*, don't drop me, please.'

Mooma was staring at the black statue on the cart and didn't seem to hear. Then she shook her head and glared at Grandpa Werewolf.

'That's mean of you, Grimbeard. What good is a statue of Armando to me? My sorrow was too great for my heart. I even forgot what it was. But now I remember and that hurts even more!' With a jolt, she turned back to the chasm.

'*Wrow!*' growled Alfie.

'No!' Tim and Noura cried in one voice.

'Mooma, wait,' crunched a deep voice, a stony voice, a gritty voice of granite. Mooma stiffened. Alfie peered past her elbow at the statue of Armando. The voice had come from the statue, he was sure of it. But . . . how?

Everyone was looking at the statue. Mum and Dad and the orphans too.

'See, my statue wants to live,' Dad whispered. 'I had to hack him out before full moon. And I managed.'

'I heard it too,' Tim said happily. 'Or is Grandpa Werewolf a secret ventriloquist?'

The statue of Armando was still standing motionless on the trolley. Alfie saw Mooma waver. She looked at Grandpa Werewolf.

'Did I hear right, Grimbeard? Was that *his* voice? Is it possible that …'

Leo pushed the trolley a little further until it was close to the edge. Mooma turned around. Now she was holding Alfie with just one hand around his ankle so that Alfie was dangling upside down over the chasm. It didn't make him feel any safer. Mooma stretched her other hand out to the statue.

'Armando?' she whispered. One claw touched the statue. She stroked the black stone.

In that instant a bright moonbeam hit that very spot and a shudder passed through the statue. The head jerked. *CRACK!* The rock started to split open. *CRACK!* It burst open in another place. Cracks spread like little rivers from top to bottom all over the statue. There were grinding and crunching sounds. Little by little, pieces of stone started to fall to the ground. The statue was slowly crumbling away. Everyone watched breathlessly. Even Alfie was holding his breath.

'Look,' Tim whispered. 'Something is coming out of the stone.'

'Not something,' Noura said, 'someone.'

Alfie stared at the figure in the black cape,

standing there between the lumps of rock. He looked surprised, as if he had just woken up. His face was pale. His hair was grey. His eyes were red.

'Thunderous thundering!' growled Leo. 'There be a vam-pirate in that stone. Like a birdy beast in a neaster egg!'

Dad sniffed with emotion. 'My work of art is really alive. This is the most beautiful reward an artist can have. I can retire now.'

'Not quite yet, dear,' Mum whispered. 'First we have to rescue Alfie. That crazy old werewolf is still capable of anything!'

Alfie breathed out. They hadn't forgotten him!

Grandpa Werewolf was the only one who didn't seem surprised. He just nodded.

'Exactly. This is how it was meant to happen. Welcome back, Armando the Grey.'

Armando looked at Mooma and smiled. There were two black holes in his smile where the dentist had pulled his fangs.

'Mooma!' he said in a voice that sounded

a little rocky. 'I have mithed you *tho* much. You're ath beautiful ath ever.'

'Hee-hee,' Leo giggled quietly.

Armando struggled to raise his arms. He seemed to want to give Mooma a hug.

'Thorry, for lithping like thith.'

Leo held his paw in front of his jaws. 'Hee-hee-hee.'

'What is it, Leo?' Tim asked.

'Oh, that just be a privatical joke of Leo's.'

Mooma stood as still as a rock. A very cautious smile gradually appeared on her face. It was as if the sun was slowly rising. As if something inside of her was thawing. Alfie held his breath again.

Hold on to me! he thought. Don't drop me!

Almost imperceptibly, Mooma's enormous body changed shape. It grew less angular, softer.

'Armando, it's really you!'

'*Wrow*,' Alfie asked, 'could you please let go of me now?' He was still dangling over

194

the chasm. 'I mean, could you please put me down gently on the ground?'

Mooma looked sideways at Alfie. 'Oh, yes, you poor werewolf orphan. I'll—'

Just then her foot slipped. The rocky edge of the cliff was slippery from all the rain. Mooma's legs shot out from under her.

'No!'

One cry, coming from everyone's lips. Grandpa Werewolf grabbed his head.

'This wasn't supposed to happen,' he mumbled.

Mooma fell. She disappeared over the edge of the cliff, dragging Alfie with her.

44

A Good Memory

'Alfie!' Mum and Noura screamed together.

For a moment everyone stared at the cliff in shock. Mooma was gone and Alfie had disappeared with her. Noura stood frozen beside Tim. Leo's jaw dropped. The orphans grabbed each other in dismay.

'It's my fault,' Olga cried. 'It's all my fault. They've fallen to their deaths.'

Then something incredible happened. Armando leapt off the trolley and hurled himself over the edge of the cliff, his cloak flapping around his body like black wings. It happened so fast that all anyone saw was a black flash. In an instant he'd disappeared. It seemed as if time had stood still. No one knew what to do.

Then Grandpa Werewolf walked slowly over to the edge of the cliff.

'Oh, no,' Noura said. 'Is Grandpa Werewolf going to jump over the cliff too? Are we all supposed to do it or what?'

But Grandpa Werewolf just stood at the edge. He turned back and beckoned.

'Come here, quick,' he said, pointing into the depths with his umbrella. 'Fortunately Armando has a good memory. He remembered that vampires are very special creatures. Sometimes they change into bats and they can also fly . . .'

Everybody ran to the cliff and looked over the edge. There below, floating in the moonlight, was Armando, close to the cliff face. His arms were spread wide and he was flapping his arms.

Hanging beneath him was Mooma, with her paws wrapped around his legs. And Alfie

was there too. He was holding tight to one of Mooma's feet.

'*Wrow*, it's OK. I'm still alive.'

Armando was looking up with a worried expression. When he saw Grandpa Werewolf he smiled.

'Grimbeard, old fellow, give uth a paw, will you? Thith ith a heavy load for an old lithping vampire. I can't get them up all by mythelff.'

'Hee-hee,' Leo giggled. 'Hold on. Leo be giving you a paw.'

Grandpa Werewolf handed Leo the umbrella. 'Your turn, Leo. But there's nothing to laugh about, you know.'

'Sorry, Grandpa, Leo be having a privatical joke.' Leo lay down flat on the edge of the cliff. 'Keeps up the good workings. Here be Leo with his helping paw.' He stuck the umbrella down over the edge as far as he could reach and Armando stretched his hand up as far as he could reach. He just managed to grab the handle of the umbrella.

'Got it.'

Quickly Leo hauled up the umbrella. Five seconds later everyone was standing on the cliff top.

Everyone hugged Alfie: Noura, Mum, Tim, Dad, Grandpa Werewolf, even Leo. And Mooma cuddled Armando. They were all relieved and overjoyed. Only the orphans were looking worried.

'What's going to happen to us now?' Olga whispered. 'Do we have to go back to the icy cellar?'

Igor shook his head angrily. 'I don't want to go back. I'd rather jump over that cliff right away.'

'Not me,' Inouk said. 'I'll run away really fast. Now!'

Just then Mooma's big paw grabbed him by the scruff of the neck. She lifted Inouk up and pressed her hairy cheek against his muzzle.

'Mooma's dear werewolf orphans. Mooma is so happy her heart has thawed. Now you can stay with Mooma and Armando for ever. In the Arma-Mooma Werewolf Orphanage.

A warm home where you can grow up safely. Where it's fun and cheerful!'

The orphans looked at each other.

'You mean we'll never have to go back into the cellar again?' Ashanti asked.

Armando laid an arm over Mooma's shoulder.

'That ith really true,' he said. 'We'll look affter you really well. I promith!'

'Hee-hee,' giggled Leo.

'Cool,' said Igor. 'Then we'll have a werewolf mother and a vampire father. Almost no one has that.'

The orphans jumped up and down, threw their heads back and howled at the moon for joy. Only Olga looked at Alfie unhappily. For a moment Alfie hesitated.

Am I still angry? he thought. No, my anger has disappeared. I'm much too happy that we've been saved. He smiled at Olga.

Gradually a smile appeared on her muzzle too. Then she leapt into the huddle of orphans and howled along with the others.

'Hooray, we've got a vampire dad and a

werewolf mum,' they sang with raspy werewolf voices.

Tim's father gave a jealous sigh. 'I wish I had a werewolf mum and a vampire dad. That would be really different! And I really love things to be different.'

Thwack!

'Ow!' Dad grabbed his ear.

Grandpa Werewolf grinned at him. 'Did I do that? Oh, well, you'd better stop moaning then. Otherwise I'll whack you on the other ear too.'

Dad rubbed his ear miserably. 'OK, Grandpa.'

Loud laughter rose up over the trees.

45

Secrets

'Look, Alfie.' Grandpa Werewolf pointed at the wall with the trees full of photos and names. The two of them were sitting alone in the Secret Room and the moon was shining in through the tall windows.

'You see the third tree from the left? They're all ancestors of yours. And you see that young man with the hat?'

'Grimbeard,' Alfie said. 'Is that really you, Grandpa?'

Grandpa Werewolf nodded. 'Definitely. That's me as a youngster. And the pretty

young lady next to me is Mooma.'

'*Wrow*, that's incredible,' Alfie growled. 'Is Grimbeard your real name? I never knew that, Grandpa.'

The old werewolf gave a growling laugh. 'How could you, Alfie? Grimbeard is my secret werewolf name. The WSO gives one to every werewolf. One day you'll get one too.'

Alfie scratched his head. '*Wrow*, what's WSO stand for, Grandpa?'

'Werewolf Secret Organization. They're the ones who pick up orphaned werewolves all over the world. They bring them here, to the werewolf orphanage. The WSO keeps the werewolf family trees in this room up to date too.'

'And the photos? How did they get one of me?'

Grandpa Werewolf chuckled. 'The WSO has secret members in every country. They send in photos of every new werewolf cub.'

Alfie looked at him. 'Are you one of those members?'

'You've figured it out, Alfie,' said Grandpa Werewolf.

Alfie studied his family tree more closely. '*Wrow*, there's Leo too. Noura's not on it.'

Grandpa Werewolf pointed at an empty spot next to Alfie's photo.

'That's right, Alfie. That's her spot. Maybe you can ask her for a photo one day? And give it to me without telling anyone. Because this is all top secret and it has to stay that way. You understand that?'

Alfie nodded. '*Wrow*, I'll take care of it, Grandpa Werewolf.'

'Excellent.' Grandpa Werewolf stood up.

'Come on, we'll go and join the others.'

They walked out of the Secret Room and into the hall with the werewolf portraits looking down on them. Their hair was even longer now and their ears were pointier.

'They're weird paintings,' Alfie said. 'It's as if they change at full moon.'

'They do,' said Grandpa Werewolf. 'Paintings of werewolves are like that sometimes.'

Suddenly a gust of wind rustled his fur. The song wind whispered down the hall.

> *A vampire's pain can end as well*
> *Although it lasted very long*
> *That was the story I had to tell*
> *This is the end of Armando's song*

Alfie and Grandpa Werewolf smiled at each other for a moment, then walked on. At the kitchen door, Alfie paused.

'*Wrow*, one last question, Grandpa. Why did you shout out that I was Mooma's grandson?'

For a second, Grandpa Werewolf seemed to blush under the hair on his cheeks.

'Mmmm, because you are, Alfie.'

Alfie couldn't believe what Grandpa was saying.

'But how can I be? I mean, who . . . what . . . how?'

Grandpa Werewolf leant on his umbrella. 'A long time ago Mooma and I were in love with each other for a while.'

'You?' Alfie couldn't imagine Grandpa Werewolf being in love. And definitely not with Mooma. Although . . . he thought of the photo of the pretty young woman. *'Wrow!'*

Grandpa Werewolf nodded. 'It's true. It didn't last that long, but we did have a baby: your real mother.' Grandpa Werewolf sighed. 'Then Armando showed up. Mooma fell in love with him. So deeply that she immediately forgot all about me. I took our daughter away with me and brought her up by myself.'

Alfie stared at Grandpa Werewolf. 'So . . .

so Mooma is actually . . .'

'Yes, Alfie. Mooma is Grandma
Werewolf.'

46

Surprise

Alfie gulped. '*Wrow*, what a . . . surprise. Grandma Mooma! Does . . . my real mother know too?'

Cheerful sounds were coming from behind the kitchen door.

'She knows, but she doesn't want anything else to do with werewolves. She's not a werewolf herself and neither is your father. You know that they abandoned you.'

Alfie nodded. 'That's why I'm lucky enough to live with a family as great as Tim's.'

Grandpa Werewolf grinned. 'Exactly!'

'*Wrow*, shall I tell Mooma myself? That it's really true that I'm her grandson?'

'That sounds like a good idea,' Grandpa Werewolf growled, pushing open the door. Everyone was sitting in the large kitchen of the werewolf orphanage talking and laughing. A big fire was burning in the fireplace and everyone was almost dry again. The full moon was shining in through a window and casting a cosy light over the kitchen table. Mum was making tea for Tim, Dad and herself, and Mooma had got a few raw, bloody steaks out of the fridge.

The orphans were sitting around the kitchen table with Tim and Noura. Alfie sat down next to Noura.

'*Wrow*, Noura, could you give me a photo of yourself sometime?'

Noura blushed and giggled. 'What? Oh . . . sure, if you like.'

Alfie grinned and gave Grandpa Werewolf the thumbs-up. Tim looked at Inouk, the North Pole werewolf. He had a white coat like Alfie's and blood-red eyes.

'*We'll never go back to the icy cellar,*' he sang. '*Mooma's promised us that.*'

'Absolutely,' growled Mooma, who had come up behind them and put a dish of steak down on the table. 'I'm going to nail the icy cellar shut. It belongs to the days when Mooma wasn't herself any more. But now I've found myself again and I only want to see happy, cheerful werewolf orphans. Dig in, everyone. The steaks are juicy, and nice and raw. Just the way you like them.' She looked around. 'Is everyone happy?'

'Absolutedly,' Leo shouted, digging his teeth into a hefty steak. Armando the Grey was standing in a corner of the room talking to Tim's father.

'I'm so proud of you,' Dad beamed. 'You've turned out so well. It cost me grit, sweat and tears, but you're a wonderful work of art!'

'Yeth and thank you very much for hacking me out of that rock,' Armando said. He waved at Mooma and sucked something red up out of a glass with a straw. 'Juth fabulouth thweetheart,' he said. 'I feel juth fine after all thothe yearth ath a dumb pieth of rock.'

Leo screamed with laughter and rolled over the floor. Everyone gaped at him.

'Leo, what are you laughing about the whole time?' Alfie asked. Leo sat up, looked at Armando and burst out laughing again.

'Sorry,' he finally growled. 'Leo can't be helping it. It all be cause of that vam-pirate.'

'What exactly do you mean, Leo?' Grandpa Werewolf said. 'Be clear for once.'

'Juth thay ekthackly what you have to thay,' said Armando. Leo roared with laughter, pounding his knees and pointing at the vampire.

'He be nice enough, but . . . he talk so funnified. That makes Leo chuckuluckle the whole time. That be tickling Leo's funny-boney.'

Everyone burst out laughing, but that was something Leo didn't understand.

'Why youse be laughing so hardly?' he asked.

And that just made them laugh even harder.

Another

ALFIE
THE
WEREWOLF

adventure

Birthday Surprise

Alfie is no ordinary boy –
at full moon he transforms
into a werewolf!

It's Alfie's birthday and he's turning more
than just a year older. Something strange is
happening to him. First comes fur …
then claws … and then a TAIL. Before he
knows it, Alfie's a furry white werewolf!

He's going to have to get used to his new
wolfish lifestyle, and stay away from next
door's chickens … who knew turning
seven would be this scary?

Another

ALFIE THE WEREWOLF

adventure

Full Moon

Alfie is no ordinary boy –
at full moon he transforms
into a werewolf!

Alfie is on a school trip for two nights
of campfires, ghost stories and a spooky
outing into eerie Sulphur Forest.
The children aren't scared, but perhaps
they should be – something strange
is lurking amongst the trees, and what's
more ... there's a full moon
and Alfie's on the loose!

Another

ALFIE
~ THE ~
WEREWOLF

adventure

Silvertooth

Alfie is no ordinary boy –
at full moon he transforms
into a werewolf!

Alfie's happy days living with
Tim's family are over when a
mysterious stranger turns up.
Soon, Alfie's trapped in a cage
with a grouchy vampire and a
mysterious creature called a
scoffle. Will he find a way to
escape before the scoffle
wakes up?

Another

ALFIE
THE
WEREWOLF

adventure

Wolf Wood

Alfie is no ordinary boy –
at full moon he transforms
into a werewolf!

Wolf Wood has been home to
generations of werewolves and
hides an important werewolf secret
… But when Alfie discovers plans to
destroy the wood, the werewolves
are in danger. Can Alfie save Wolf
Wood – before it gets turned into
blocks of flats!

Another

ALFIE
~ THE ~
WEREWOLF

adventure

The Evil Triplets

Alfie is no ordinary boy –
at full moon he transforms
into a werewolf!

Alfie's crazy, werewolf-hating
neighbour, Mrs Chalker, is back ...
and this time there's three of her!
Alfie must be on his guard and when
he spots the Mrs Chalker look-alikes
acting suspiciously he knows they're
up to something ... but what?